ANGEL BLOOD

By
J.E. Taylor

JET-Fueled Fiction
Angel Blood © 2024 J.E. Taylor
2nd Edition

For additional information contact:
www.JETaylor75.com
Cover Art by Cora Graphics
www.coragraphics.it

ANGEL BLOOD

Someone is murdering people, draining them dry, and the police suspect it may be a vampire. When the captain of the York police department turns to Tom Ryan and his paranormal investigation agency for help, Tom takes one look at the crime scene photos and knows the killer isn't a blood sucker.

Tom and his business partner compare the murders with a list of angel descendants and a chilling pattern is confirmed. Angel bloodlines are being extinguished, and there are only a handful left between the killer's hunting ground and their family in York.

They must stop the assassin before he can cross off any more names on his hit list.

Chapter 1

THE TELEPHONE INTERRUPTED US, and I gazed into Raven's eyes, stilling my hips. The way her hair fanned out around her made her look like she had an ornate halo made of red fire, and it fueled my slow burn. The chances we had to screw around were not as abundant as they had been when we were first married. Since Hannah was born, it was catching a quickie whenever we could, and tonight our daughter had gone to bed early after a fun day at the beach. You can bet your ass we took full advantage of the time.

Until now.

"Don't answer it," she whispered, and her legs wrapped tighter around mine, her hips circled, and that partial smile and sparkle in her eyes nearly made me reconsider.

"I have to," I said. Of course the words coming out of my mouth were garbled, despite the clarity of them in my mind. Raven understood and her sigh conveyed her disdain.

"Ya," I mumbled into the receiver.

"There's water everywhere. What do I do?" The panicked voice of my brother filled the line.

"Huh?" I pushed onto my knees, still coupled with Raven, and I put the phone on speaker.

"Water. She's like a fucking geyser," CJ said, and I locked my gaze with Raven, pressing my lips against the smile.

"Get her to the hospital, you ass," Raven said. "She's in labor."

I grinned down at her and circled my hips. My wife's Irish lilt turned me on something fierce, and even though I knew she wanted to jump out of bed and run to the hospital for our nephew's birth, I wasn't in any rush.

"Oh. Shit." CJ said with a laugh. "Okay, my brain isn't quite working right now."

"Go. We'll meet you there," Raven said, and the dial tone filled the room.

"Not 'til we finish this," I signed, and my hips started that slow grind she usually loved. However, her features turned to annoyance.

"Your brother is an idiot," she said. "Valerie needs someone who knows what they are doing."

I shook my head. "We have time," I said, and tapped my wrist so the gist of what I was trying to say would be transmitted.

Raven rolled her eyes and then her hips. "Fine, but hurry up," she whispered.

I stilled my hips and sent her a head tilt, wrinkling my brow. I wanted this to last. Besides, no one was there to hold our hands when Hannah was born. CJ was in a coma and everyone else was so preoccupied with life that we were on our own. If I got through the birth of my daughter, CJ would get through this, whether or not we were there.

"Tom," she started.

I didn't need the words. I already had a line into her thoughts ever since CJ supercharged me. My wife was torn between wanting to enjoy this and wanting to go to the hospital, which meant any chance of her enjoying this was out the window.

"Fine," I said with a sigh, and pulled out, accepting the burn of frustration that filled me as the price I had to pay for loving a woman whose heart was big enough to cover this half of the hemisphere.

I knew she loved me, but Valerie was her best friend, and she thought my brother was inept in almost every way. The truth of the matter was CJ Ryan was a Mensa-level genius with the power to destroy the universe.

"You know I love you." She grabbed my arm as I climbed off the bed.

I nodded, opting for the more simple head bob than trying to speak without a tongue or with my hands, which were now occupied with pulling on clothing.

"I promise, I'll make it up to you," she said as she shuffled through the pile of garments on the chair for something suitable to wear.

Yeah, I'd heard that before, and sent her an elevated eyebrow even as my eyes took in her incredible curves. I let my gaze linger, and the hunger I always seemed to have for her stirred.

Raven stopped with the shirt half on and blew me a kiss before she busied herself with clothing the rest of her naked form. My options were easy. Shorts, a t-shirt, and my beach sandals, considering the early heat wave.

My gaze jumped from the time blinking a few minutes before midnight to the calendar. I zeroed in on tomorrow's date. July seventh.

A chill saturated my body.

My father's birthday was July seventh, and it looked like his namesake would share that same date.

"Are you okay?" Raven's question pulled my gaze from the calendar, and I met her blue-eyed stare.

Shrugging, I pointed to the object of the goose flesh now peppering my skin.

She looked between the calendar and me. "Yeah?"

"Tomorrow is my father's birthday," I signed.

Her gaze drifted back to the calendar, her skin rippling the same way mine had. "Well, let's hope our nephew's future differs vastly from your father's," she said, pulling a laugh and a nod from me.

Ty Alexander Ryan had raised me as his own, even though I was sired by another man and shared the womb with his natural son. He had given me everything a kid could ever ask for while he was alive, from love to self-confidence, and everything in between. We lived a blessed life for many years, and then Steve Williams stepped into the picture.

My father's death rocked both CJ and me, and everything since then had been hard. At first, I blamed Steve. If he hadn't come into our lives, my father and mother would still be alive. At least, that's what I tried to convince myself for years, and I rebelled in every fashion; pushing Steve to the edge more than once while he did his best to become our default dad.

I'm not sure I would have been able to move past the blame had I not had the benefit of seeing my father on a daily basis in angel form. He stood watch over Steve for years, and while CJ could hear him talking to Steve, I could see him. His pride in us, and his disappointment when I fucked up, was as visible as Steve's was.

I shook away the wave of memories that cropped to the surface; burying them in the overwhelming flurry of Raven's thoughts already accosting my mind, and stepped into the bathroom to run a brush through my hair. My light blue eyes peered back at me, and I tried to get my black hair to look decent and not like we had been fucking around. After a few swipes of the brush I gave up and relinquished the spot to Raven. Her rush out of the house included a retouch of her makeup, and I went to collect our sleeping three-year-old.

Chapter 2

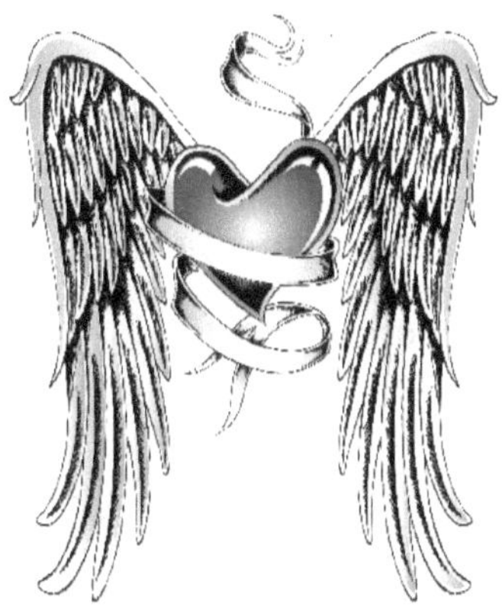

THEY LET RAVEN INTO the room for the birth, while I sat out in the waiting area, entertaining Hannah with *Rumble in the Jungle* on our iPad. I knew we'd pay for this interruption in her sleep schedule at some inopportune moment tomorrow, but for now, she was content.

It didn't take Hannah long to yawn, and she curled up in my lap with her thumb stuck in her mouth and her blanket wrapped around her. She finally faded into sleep around two and I set her down on one of the couches.

I sent out a couple of text messages. I knew neither Steve nor Damian would pick it up before dawn, but on the off-chance CJ hadn't notified them, at least they'd wake to some happy news. Before I could slip the phone back in my pocket, it buzzed, and I glanced down at the new text from Steve.

On our way. I sighed and glanced at Hannah, feeling that old twinge of jealousy again. I gritted my teeth, inhaled deeply, then slowly exhaled to let go of the burn. No one had immediately come when we were in the same situation. My phone buzzed again, and I glanced at the second text from Steve. *We need to talk.*

Surprise raked its nails across my chest, and my eyebrows rose.

I had just typed out the word why when the door to the waiting room opened. I glanced up and forgot about pressing the send button.

"Steve said I might find you here," Captain O'Keefe from the York Police Department stepped into the room looking like he hadn't slept in days. His dark eyes, as tired as they looked, sharpened as they met mine.

I stiffened. Usually, when Captain O'Keefe came looking for me, I was in a shitload of trouble. Especially in the middle of the night. However, the look in his eyes wasn't the usual confrontational scowl I was used to, and I didn't need to do a mind scan this time to get that he wasn't here to haul me in.

"What can I do for you?" I signed.

He stared at my hands and his cheeks turned red. "I still can't follow sign language."

I swiped the iPad off the table and typed my question along with a plea for him to keep his voice low, so we didn't wake Hannah. When I turned the tablet in his direction, he glanced beyond me at the couch with a small smile and a nod. Instead of talking out loud, he took the tablet from me and started typing.

I focused on him, draining the answers right out of his mind, so when he handed me the iPad, I only had to scan the text confirming what he wanted. I glanced over at him.

"You want my help?" I said. Of course, what verbally came out was a complete bastardization of the question, but Captain O'Keefe got it.

"Steve said this is the type of thing your company investigates." He handed me the file he carried.

I inhaled and glanced at him before flipping the folder open. The picture on the top of the pile chilled me to the bone, and I wished I had a blanket like Hannah, if only to hide the rash of gooseflesh now standing out on my arms and legs.

The girl in the photo was splayed out and pale to the point of being almost ashen. Even the color in her eyes had faded. I shuffled to the next picture and sat straight up. Two distinct puncture wounds, far enough apart to suggest teeth, speckled her carotid artery.

Shuffling through the dozen photos brought the same results, and I turned them over, placing them face down on the chair next to me before I leaned forward and read each of the reports. The fundamental similarity in all the cases was the bodies had been drained of blood. I closed the folder, placing it on the pile of photos before I glanced at Captain O'Keefe.

"What's your conclusion?" I tapped out on my iPad and took a moment to pull up some of Damian's memories. The bite signature was all wrong for the crazed vampires he encountered, and my limited exposure matched his, but that didn't mean it wasn't something supernatural.

Captain O'Keefe licked his lips and let out a soft laugh. "I don't know what to think," he said, and I raised an eyebrow, challenging him because his thoughts danced around the vampire lore like a moth to a forest fire. "At least nothing logical," he added, and busied himself with putting the photos back in the folder.

"What exactly do you want from us?" I asked. I also projected the words into his head, and his eyes snapped up to mine in confusion.

"I'm not sure. Steve said you investigated… paranormal activity?" His voice carried the disdain I could feel radiating from him.

I nodded. "But you don't believe in that shit," I said, again transmitting so the words would be clear over my tongue-less banter.

Again, he blinked, paling a fraction, and my lips twitched against the smirk that wanted to appear. His gaze dropped to the folder. "I don't know what to believe."

I typed out three words on my iPad and handed it to him.

Monsters are real.

He stared at the text and slowly handed the iPad back.

The Windwalker, The Slasher. The butcher in Georgia. All monsters, and all very real.

I handed him the newly typed text.

"But with all those killers, there was some sort of evidence. In these cases, there is nothing. Zero. Just bodies drained completely of blood." He strained to keep his voice from rising above a whisper, but the exasperation rang clear.

"And you think it's a vampire?" Of course, my words were more or less grunt-like without my tongue. I didn't send the thought, either.

Captain O'Keefe's brow creased. He didn't have a clue of what I said.

Instead of typing what I tried to say, I stared at him and projected my next thought loud enough to draw a wince.

"Stop beating around the bush. What exactly do you think is killing people?"

Captain O'Keefe's eyes widened before he started blinking furiously and glancing around for the source of the words in his mind.

"It's me, you dumb shit." I crossed my arms and leaned back in the chair as he paled. For a fleeting moment, I enjoyed the shock skittering over his features like an army of ants, and then I second-guessed my wisdom as he retreated into the back of his seat like I was a deadly disease.

"Look," I started, forming words with both my mouth and my mind. "I recently acquired the ability to project my thoughts. I know it's a little freaky, but it certainly helps with what I lack in diction, don't you think?" I offered a half-hearted tilt of my lips.

"I just... I just have never..." His brain was short-circuiting with this new twist and his gaze dropped to the file in his hands while he processed. He had heard a few stories about my ability to see ghosts, but he discounted those as drug-induced hallucinations or overly active imaginations. But now, with this manifestation, he started looking at all the other tall tales. His gaze slowly rose to mine.

"Is this why you opened a paranormal investigation business?"

I gave him a shrug. "Some of those stories aren't too far from the truth." I allowed, and his eyebrows arched. "I can see ghosts."

"Like the kid in *The Sixth Sense*?" he asked, his eyes as wide as Hannah's when we tell her she can pick out whatever she wants at the Goldenrod's candy counter.

I chuckled and glanced at Hannah before returning his questioning stare. "I guess, and yeah, it makes me a little bit more qualified to hunt ghosts."

"What about this?" He raised the folder. "Do you investigate things like this?"

My smile faded. "I'm not a cop, or a forensic specialist, for that matter."

"But do you look into shit like this?" he hissed, his frustration at my lack of an answer finally bubbling up.

"Captain, how many unsolved cases are there in York?"

He stared at me. There was only one I knew of. Sarah, Steve's ex-partner, had disappeared from an active crime scene at CJ's house. That one would never be solved, because Sarah had been kidnapped by Lucifer as a bargaining chip. Unfortunately, it hadn't worked out all that well for her and there was nothing left for the law to find.

"Only one," he said, and he held up the file. "But this is happening in the Portland area. Not York. They seem to think we have an inside track on catching madmen after the Windwalker case and wanted our help before they got the FBI involved." He sighed and ran his hand over his face. "So, I called your father."

"And Steve sent you to me."

Captain O'Keefe nodded.

"You remember what happened the last time I tried to intervene in an active case?" I couldn't help but ask. After all, he was the one who was positive I was the Windwalker, and he was the one who was ready to throw away the key after they arrested me. He nearly had me tried and on death row before I was even read my rights. Granted, I had been a frequent visitor to the York Police department's juvenile holding tank, but that time, he put me in with the adults and I nearly became someone's bitch.

His eyes dropped to the ground. "Yes."

"So, what exactly do you want us to do?"

He bit his lip and the flurry of thought in his mind nearly drowned out the soft, "I don't know." When he slid his gaze to mine, I got it. He couldn't wrap his mind around the existence of vampires; of a creature so cunning, that kills so completely, and leaves no trace. Captain O'Keefe was afraid of the unknown, and after all the crazy shit I've seen in the last few years, I'd say he had a damned good reason to be scared.

"What if I told you I wasn't sure what did that?" I jutted my chin towards the file. "I'm not ready to rule out a human killer. After all, the Windwalker had stumped you all on a couple of his crime scenes."

His eyelids fluttered as his mind wrapped fully around the conversations. "So, there are things out there..." He trailed off.

"You don't want to know the answer to that." I didn't give him any leeway, but his lips pressed together at my tone, even as his brain shrouded with doubt.

"I need to know."

"Trust me, you really don't. I know enough to freak you out for a fucking lifetime, and I'm not inclined to share." I pointed to the file. "We'll help you with that, but if it turns out to be something we specialize in..." I let my eyebrows rise with the lilt in my voice, trailing off in more of a question than a statement.

Captain O'Keefe didn't take the bait to complete the sentence. He just stared at me, waiting for me to finish.

"If it turns out to be our specialty, you have to let us take care of it."

"Oh, no," he started, and I put my hand up, stopping him.

"If it turns out to be your specialty, we can back you up if you need us, but if it's in our realm, you are ill suited to be anywhere near us when we take whatever it is down."

"I can't just let you put a stake through their heart," he stammered, and I burst out laughing.

"That's not how you kill a vampire," I said, thinking about the toxins in my blood. If he ever witnessed what my blood did to those parasites, he would probably check himself into the loony bin. "A platinum bullet to the brain will do it."

His incessant blink pulled a smirk to my lips.

"Sunshine will toast their ass, too."

His tense features smoothed over as the more familiar lore settled a little comfort in his bones.

"Will they... become vampires?" He held up the file.

"No."

"If I got bit..."

"You'd probably die. Vampire venom is poisonous."

"I can't believe I'm having this conversation," he muttered under his breath.

"I've known about ghosts all my life, but this shit, this fucked me up something fierce." I couldn't help the grin, or the heat in my cheeks at the admission.

He dropped the file onto the table and rubbed his face. "I must be exhausted to even entertain this crap," he said and sent a tired smile my way. "So... you're going to be an uncle?"

The change of subject brought a natural smile to my face. "Yes." I accompanied the word with the hand signal out of habit. It was one of the few sign language motions that O'Keefe knew.

He sat silent for a few minutes, his gaze drifting to my daughter. "Are you going to have more?"

Raven and I had talked about it, but so far nothing had happened in the baby-making department. However, this wasn't a subject I wanted to discuss on the heels of murder and vampires. I just gave a non-committal shrug and left it at that.

He stood to leave. "Why don't you stop in at the station when you have some time," he said and headed for the door. He paused and glanced back at me. "How does one get platinum bullets?"

The grin that surfaced held some of my good humor. "You need to make them."

"Oh." He seemed genuinely disappointed, like I should have been able to supply him with a '1-800-bullets' manufacturer. "Well, I'll see you later."

I waved, and the door closed behind him. My smile faded at the thought of another killer within a hundred miles of this place. Especially if it was of the supernatural persuasion.

Chapter 3

WEIGHT SHIFTED ON MY lap, pulling me out of sleep. My eyes snapped open to the unfamiliar surroundings as Hannah snuggled into me. I glanced at the clock on the wall and sat up a little straighter. It was quarter after seven and I wasn't alone in the waiting room. Steve and Jennifer sat opposite me; Steve's dark hair looked almost as disheveled as mine did last night, and his reading glasses magnified the dark circles under his eyes. For the life of me, I couldn't understand how anything he was reading could stick. Jennifer's chestnut hair fell over his shoulder as she leaned on him, her eyes at half-mast and the paperback in her hand long forgotten.

"No word?" My voice cracked as I spoke and startled both of them. I didn't bother sending the thought. Jennifer and Steve knew me well enough to understand my words, even though to most people it was just a jumble of sounds that made little sense.

Steve glanced over the top of the newspaper and shook his head.

I shifted Hannah back to the couch and slipped into the restroom attached to the waiting area. One look in the mirror told me enough about how little sleep I'd actually gotten, and I couldn't imagine Raven got any more than I did. A splash of cold water seemed to snap my senses back in order, and I dried my face before stepping back into the waiting room.

It was almost as if we had timed it. The moment I opened the door from the restroom, CJ opened the door to the waiting room with the biggest grin I've seen in years. His gaze met mine, and I smiled back. I remember that instant rush of excitement and awe the moment I became a father, and I crossed, getting to him before Steve, and giving him a hug accompanied by the usual back slap.

"Congratulations!" I broadcast, sharing his enthusiasm, and then relinquished my spot to Steve and Jennifer.

"So?" I asked after hugs were given all around.

"A healthy boy at seven pounds, seven ounces and seventeen inches long." He smiled and met my gaze.

A chill encased my spine, but I kept my smile intact.

"Born at seven-o-seven this morning."

"Kind of freaky," I mumbled, and his grin got wider and was accompanied by a mischievous sparkle in his eyes that reminded me of the mid-summer sun-drenched Atlantic.

"Yeah. Looks like sevens all around. And it was like he waited until that exact time to be born. Want to come see your nephew?" he asked, bypassing everyone else and meeting my gaze.

I turned to Jennifer.

"I'll watch Hannah, go," she said before I could ask if she would watch my daughter.

I stepped out into the hall with my brother and gave him a pat on the back. "How's Valerie?" I asked.

"Tired, but she is happier than I've ever seen her." He pushed the door open, allowing me to step inside first.

Valerie had the same radiance that Raven had after Hannah was born. Her dark hair was wet with sweat and wisps still clung to her face. Her tired eyes held the smile reflected on her lips, and I couldn't help but smile back. I still do not know how mothers can look so exhausted and radiant at the same time. I glanced down at the newest addition to our family before trading a glance with Raven, and she sent me a happy grin.

CJ stepped closer to the bed.

"Meet your nephew, Alex," he said and took the baby from Valerie.

"Alex?" I asked, meeting his gaze.

"Ty Alexander Ryan." He handed the baby to me. "We decided to call him Alex instead of Ty."

I stared down into the bright blue eyes that were a carbon copy of my father's, and I understood the aversion to calling him Ty. They wanted to give him a fighting chance and not saddle him with the stigma that came with his grandfather's name.

"Alex, meet your Uncle Tom," CJ added, stepping close and looking down into the baby's eyes.

There wasn't a thing I wouldn't do for my daughter, and that same fierce parental instinct wound its way around my heart when the child's gaze met mine. I smiled and said one of the few words I could articulate clearly. "Hi."

CJ cleared his throat, and I glanced up at him.

"We'd like you and Raven to be his godparents."

My eyebrows rose. I wasn't in any way a devout Christian, and Raven certainly wasn't, either, so why he was choosing us was beyond me. My shock must have shown because he chuckled.

"Maybe guardian is a better word?"

My brow smoothed out, and I smirked and nodded, bringing my gaze back to his son. "He's got your eyes," I said, conveying the words with my thoughts.

"Yeah," CJ said, and I turned my attention to Valerie.

"How are you doing?" I signed with one hand.

"I'm doing pretty good," she said, but it was promptly followed by a yawn, and I met Raven's gaze. She nodded toward the door.

"We should let Steve and Jen see the baby," she said, as if the head nod wasn't enough.

I relinquished the child to my brother before leaning over and planting a kiss on Valerie's cheek. "Congratulations," I said, and she smiled, hearing the thought I projected as easily as my brother. As I turned, I caught sight of the thin line of salt cutting the room in half and I brought my gaze to CJ's.

"Just covering the bases," he said softly.

My smile faded, and I nodded, making a note not to disturb the solid line when I left the room. That was another fact of our lives that I wish had remained in the darkness. We both had angel blood running through our veins and little Alex was the first of his kind, carrying the bloodlines of four archangels.

CJ's caution against a demon attack was warranted. I shivered, thinking of what Lucifer would do to that child if he ever got his greedy hands on him.

The door swung open and my partner's daughter, Grace, came running into the room, her eyes wide and her cheeks pink from breaking away from the rest of her family. She was not the typical five-year-old, by any means, and the fact she burst into the room like the place was on fire was both amusing and a little concerning. She was halfway across the room when a nurse stepped in the door.

"I'm sorry, but children are not allowed..."

Grace turned and put her hand up like a stop sign, her brow creased in irritation, but it had the desired effect. Silence overtook everyone at the child's audacity.

Damian Andreas slid next to the nurse standing in the doorway. He was as equally out of breath as his daughter, and his dark Greek features formed a mask of aggravation.

Grace turned back toward CJ, and her eyes landed on the baby in his arms. The calm that settled over the room was eerie, and I traded a glance with Raven.

The child tentatively stepped over the salt line and CJ squatted to show her his son. The silent communication between CJ and Grace had been strong since the day she was born, and today was no different. But the awe in Grace's face transformed when her gaze met the baby's.

Alex stared at her as well, and it just wasn't a normal baby stare. It reminded me of the times when Grace was his age and would look at us with such wisdom; it gave me the shivers. It was as if the child knew the secrets of the cosmos.

Grace reached for his cheek, hesitating before she touched him. Her eyes drifted to CJ's, and they were painted with such fervent adoration, I had to smile.

"Grace," Damian said as he stepped into the room, but she ignored her father.

When her fingers brushed the baby's cheek, the light I remembered Damian being bathed in the night my father died encompassed the three true trinities. Alex stared at Grace and the unyielding bond between the children formed, wrapping light strings around the two as their auras intertwined.

"Blessed be," Raven whispered, and I glanced at her. Her squinting stare told me she was seeing the same interwoven aura I was seeing.

When I glanced back, the light had already started to fade and CJ's glance met mine. He offered me a one-shouldered shrug, like he'd expected some sort of a cataclysmic event like this.

"Grace," Damian's voice rang out again, but this time, it broke the spell completely.

"What, Daddy?" Grace asked and turned, flipping her dark hair in what I could only surmise was what defiance looked like in a five-year-old.

"Only family is allowed in here," he said, reiterating what the nurse had tried to say.

Everyone's gaze drifted toward the wide-eyed nurse standing next to Damian.

"We are family," Grace said.

"Only immediate family," the nurse said, now that she regained some of her composure.

"On that note," I signed and put my hand out for Grace. She accepted my offering, but I could tell it was only because I wasn't her father, and that was further reinforced with the glare she sent in his direction, like he had initially said she couldn't go in the room.

I glanced at CJ over my shoulder before I passed through the door. He gave me his signature wave and grinned in a way I didn't quite understand, but unfortunately, I knew that look all too well. My brother had a secret. One I didn't really want to know.

Grace gave my hand a squeeze and then begrudgingly took Damian's hand, despite knowing the lecture from her dad was about to be delivered with the full force of an angry parent.

"We need to talk," I said to Damian. "Swing over when you're done here, okay?"

"Sure." he said, but both his tone and his lips were tight and the moment his gaze landed on his little girl, the tirade started.

We didn't stick around for the berating. Instead, we headed toward the waiting room to take Hannah home and give Steve and Jennifer a chance to see the new baby.

"Do you have an extra bloodstone?" I asked Raven before we entered the waiting room.

"Aye, it's woven into the small ankle bracelet I already put on the baby." She met my gaze, and I smiled, placing a kiss on her forehead as I reached for the door.

Hannah was happily playing with Damian's boys. Gabriel and Michael looked up from the coloring books and waved.

"How's Valerie?" Damian's wife, Naomi asked.

"Tired," Raven said. "It was a long night, and that boy just didn't want to come out." She covered a yawn and put her hand out for Hannah.

Hannah ignored her.

"Come on, sweetie, it's time to go," Raven said.

Jennifer stepped out of the bathroom, and I smiled in her direction.

"Your turn," I signed, and both Steve and Jennifer took off like a bolt, both of them beaming the way only grandparents can.

I focused on my daughter and crouched down next to her, hooking her chin so she had to look at me. "Time to go," I signed. She pressed her lips together and shook her head, her fiery red hair bouncing with the shake.

"Ya," I said. Lack of sleep always made her ornery, and neither of us had the tolerance this morning for a scene. I stepped away and collected our stuff, handing it all to Raven before I scooped up Hannah in my arms.

You would have thought I was murdering her with the way she was pitching a fit. I sent a shrug and uncomfortable smile in Damian's direction and carried her out into the hallway, where her shrieks echoed through the maternity ward.

By the time we got to the car, I had a scratch mark on my cheek, and I was holding my daughter in more of a bear hug than cradling her. Raven opened the back door and dumped our stuff on the floor, relinquishing the space for me to put the child in her car seat.

It's nearly impossible to bend a three-year-old who has decided she does not want to be strapped in, and finally, I let out a frustrated growl.

"Sit," I transmitted, and Hannah's eyes widened as her body behaved. The moment I had her strapped in, I closed the back door and slid into the driver's seat, more tired from the last few minutes than I was from the lack of sleep all night.

"Did you just?" Raven asked, waving her finger towards the back seat.

I rarely exercised my power over other people, but when my daughter became a devil child, I had no qualms about forcing my will upon her.

"You know that's not fair," Raven said under her breath.

"Life's not fair," I transmitted with a glare. "I can not reason with her while I'm trying to strap her into her car seat."

"I know, but there has to be a better way," she said and then chewed on her lip, signaling she had more to say, but left it alone.

I could have forced the finished thoughts from her, but I was too damned tired, and I had a case file to study. She reached for my hand, and I threaded my fingers through hers, accepting the squeeze as her way of telling me she loved me, anyway.

I pulled out, heading for home, and a nice soft mattress to catch some z's.

Chapter 4

WE WALKED INTO OUR house at a little after nine; I tucked Raven and Hannah into our bed and went into the living room. Despite how tired I was, I booted up my laptop and propped it on my lap as I stretched out on the couch.

The first thing I did was pull everything I could from the media accounts relating to the murders. There wasn't as much as I would have thought, so the Portland police were really keeping the particulars under wraps. I closed the laptop and placed it on the coffee table.

My thoughts drifted to the news accounts of the Windwalker case. It wasn't until the third death that the details leaked, but in the current case, even with the speed of information, they'd kept a cap on the information.

I rubbed my face and my eyelids dropped closed. I thought, *just a few minutes.*

Shuffling papers snapped my eyes open, and I glanced at the table and the chair beyond. Damian sat sifting through the file. He glanced up at me after a few minutes, aware that I was now awake.

"I gather this is what you wanted to discuss?"

"Ya," I said and sat up, rubbing the sleep from my eyes.

"It's not a vampire." He dropped the file on the table, and I raised my eyebrows in his direction, questioning his statement.

"I know," I signed. "I'm not convinced it's anything supernatural, but I said we'd look into it."

Damian bit his lip, glancing at the photos. "Whoever, or whatever it is, is certainly trying to make it look like the old vampire lore. But as you know, vampire attacks actually look like animal attacks when the body is found, so..." He trailed off as he looked at the names of the deceased. The cock of his head pulled my attention, and when his gaze rose, I couldn't help but shiver. "I recognize one of the names," he said, and then studied the rest.

"Well?" I asked, unable to pull any information from his mind.

"It's one of Michael's descendants."

"Coincidence?" I asked, because I couldn't fathom any other rationale.

He shrugged his shoulder. "I don't recognize the rest. But then again, I was never privy to the other angel blood lines." His gaze met mine. "We might want to have CJ take a look."

"Why?" I asked, trying to hide the sudden bloom of irritation. Any time Damian asked to bring CJ into the fold, irritation raked across my back like I wasn't good enough despite the years of pulling my weight with no supernatural advantages. Now that I was infused with some of CJ's mojo, I was just as dangerous as Damian.

"Chill, I'm not trying to bring him into the business," Damian said, putting his hands up to stop my silent rant. "When he was in heaven, he saw our ancestral bloodlines mapped from the beginning. He might recognize the names if there are any other descendants here."

I rubbed my eyes and nodded. I didn't realize just how exhausted I was, but I had to be running on empty to let that ugly sibling rivalry gene come to the surface. As if my body agreed, I yawned.

"Sorry. I'm just tired," I mumbled, projecting the thought.

"You know your brother would be an asset," he started, and I glared up at him.

I wasn't stupid. What CJ brought to the table was beyond either of our arsenal, but the fact I have something of my own, apart from my fraternal twin, brought me a sense of pride. Even if I called him in, I would be the one calling the shots. That seemed different from following in his shadow, as I had done all my life.

Damian's brow creased, and he cocked his head to the side, studying me. "You don't like your brother, do you?"

I laughed at his unwelcomed assessment. "I love my brother."

"Then why don't you want him on our team?"

We'd had this argument a few times since my brother came back from the dead, but I held my ground without much of an explanation to Damian. I knew CJ would be a hell of an asset. He has been on other cases, like what happened in New York recently, but I couldn't be delegated to the bottom rung in a business I started on my own.

"CJ would want to run things," I finally signed, meeting Damian's gaze. "He isn't much of a follower."

It was Damian's turn to chuckle, and he gave me a knowing nod. "You are probably right. I don't think either of us would appreciate that."

I shared a smile, and it tuned into another yawn.

"Did you get any sleep?"

"Just whatever I had on the couch and that wasn't enough," I said.

Damian dropped his gaze to the file and chewed his bottom lip in contemplation. "Did you want to go to the station now or tomorrow after you get some sleep?"

Raven had been up all night and if Hanna woke while I was gone, my wife would probably filet my ass, especially after Hannah's hissy fit, and the morning tension my actions already caused.

"Tomorrow," I said.

"Good. I'll see if I can find any other deaths that presented similarly, in case this isn't as localized as the cops think."

My eyebrows rose. "You think there are more deaths?"

Apprehension painted his face. "I just have a bad feeling about this one."

I knew the feeling. The lack of physical evidence at the crime scenes didn't bother me as much as the method of the kill.

Chapter 5

A SOFT CARESS ON my cheek pulled me out of sleep and I opened my eyes to meet Raven's gaze. I glanced around at the darkened room.

"What time is it?" I asked, and as always, whenever I wake from a sound sleep, I forget my speech is limited. I forget I don't have most of my tongue. Thankfully, after over ten years together, Raven understood what I muttered.

"It's a little after eight. I thought you might like to have a little dinner and then help me tuck Hannah into bed."

"I slept all day?"

She nodded. "I had a bear of a time keeping Hannah quiet, but she was more than happy to when I said she could play beauty shop."

A smirk appeared as her gaze moved from my face to my hair and back. I reached up, running my hand over my head. The sporadic tufts of hair sticking every which way told me Hannah went to town with my longer than usual locks, and I'd be peeling little rubber bands out of my scalp for the next week. I was equally amused and astounded that I slept through it.

"Oh, the hair is just the finishing touch. You need to go look in the mirror, hon."

I got up and crossed to the half-bath off the kitchen, she followed, grabbing her phone from her pocketbook, and before I saw what kind of hellish masterpiece my daughter employed, the flash went off on her phone and Raven's thinly veiled chuckle made my lips twitch into a smile.

The minute I stepped in front of the mirror, all humor turned to mortification.

"Give me that phone," I signed and reached for it. I could just see her posting it on Facebook, or worse, sending my family the photo. I looked like a painted whore, and I would never live this down if CJ got a hold of it. The bright red lipstick matched the rose blush packed onto my cheeks, but the purple and pink eye shadow just made it all a bit over the top with the dozen or so mini ponytails.

"No way!" She laughed and dodged my attempt to grab it.

"You let her do this on purpose, didn't you?" I signed, chasing after her.

She nodded in response. "You were out cold. It's your fault for not waking," she said, with that mischievous glow dancing in her eyes.

I grinned and lunged, grabbing her around the waist. She squealed, and I rubbed my face on her cheek, smearing the makeup on her with a laugh.

"Daddy!" Hannah said from the doorway, pulling my attention away from the beginning of a moment that could have ended with us stripped down to nothing and going at it on the floor.

Still holding Raven with one arm, I glanced at my daughter and pointed at my face, raising my eyebrows.

Hannah's giggle erupted. My three-year-old could bring an entire theater to laughter with her infectious giggle. I let my wife go and ran at my little girl, swept her up in my arms, and nuzzled my face in her neck with a laughing growl, smearing the makeup on her as well.

"Well, now, I think we all need to get cleaned up," Raven said, wiping her palm along her smeared cheek.

I gave Hannah a wet kiss on the cheek and planted her on the ground.

"I can eat after we tuck her in," I signed. I wasn't hungry in the least.

Raven gave me her questioning look. I guess my perpetual lack of appetite drove her insane. She needed food regularly, even if it was just a small snack. I, on the other hand, could go all day without eating when I was at the office. However, you give me a day of surfing and I could eat us out of house and home afterwards.

I smiled and corralled Hannah toward the main bathroom to clean her up. Raven followed and after we all successfully washed the makeup off; our nightly routine took over. Finish bathing Hannah, read her a book, and then tuck her in before we retreated to either the living room or bedroom. Tonight, I changed things up by heading to the kitchen to whip up a quick meal.

Raven followed me in and sat at the table. I could see her watching me in the reflection of the windows and I glanced over my shoulder, sending a smile her way.

"I still wonder how I got so lucky," she said with a sigh, as I slid my omelet onto a plate.

Grabbing the salsa, I took a seat opposite her and signed. "I'm the lucky one," before I dug in. Just the radiance in her smile alone was enough to light my fire.

"I believe you have some making up to do," I transmitted, pointing my fork at her.

Her cheeks bloomed as red as her hair, and she smiled. "I believe you are correct," she said, and licked her lips in that way that made me want to sweep the food onto the floor and take her right there. It's funny how much she can get my libido going with one innocent, or in this case, not so innocent, motion.

I sent her a wink. "Let me at least finish my meal. I have a feeling I'm going to need it."

Her laughter rang out. "So, you're expecting a little more than a two-minute interlude?" She challenged me with a raised eyebrow.

"Hell, yeah," I signed, then popped the last bite in my mouth and put the dishes in the sink with the pan, letting it soak until the morning. I turned and leaned on the side of the counter, putting on my signature grin. It always had the same effect on Raven, and she cursed me every time I purposely delivered it.

"Damn boy, you're still as hot as you were in high school," she said in that sultry Irish tone and she stood, crossing the distance to place the gentlest of kisses on my lips.

"So are you," I whispered, transmitting just as softly. I ran my fingers through her damp hair and pressed a more insistent kiss on her lips. While I only had a stub of a tongue, she still enjoyed exploring my mouth with her tongue. Her kisses always cut me off at the knees.

Everyone else I'd dated before her made me feel like a freak, but Raven never shied away from me or my lack of being able to do certain things, like kiss properly or tongue fuck, which was the usual complaint when a girl dumped me. I learned to do a few tricks in bed that made me notorious in high school, and kept girls interested for a little longer, but it never was enough for anyone else but her.

I pulled away and stared down into her deep blue eyes. "I love you." I spoke the words, and she beamed, even though they sounded like a bunch of jumbled vowels.

"I love you, too," she said. She knew my sounds, and it always gave me a sense of humbleness when she understood what was in my heart.

The connection between us was so strong that my definition of soul mate had changed drastically from those high school days. A soul mate was much deeper than just a fuckbuddy, and Raven taught me that from the beginning.

I trusted her in ways I didn't even trust my brother, and because of that, when she asked me to show her what happened in Georgia, I didn't just shut down and walk away. She wanted to know the source that continued to haunt me in my dreams.

I didn't run, but I also didn't give in to her request right away. The last thing I wanted from my wife was the pity-look. Besides, the nightmares had changed since I became a father. Instead of me on that operating table, it was Hannah. When I had those nightmares, the fear from those dreams bled into the bedroom as she rubbed my sweat ridden back, assuring me that whatever it was, it was just a nightmare.

Showing her meant reliving the experience, and I wasn't sure I could do it again, but I eventually sucked it up and allowed her to see a glimpse of the torture I'd endured. Thankfully, it was late enough that Hannah didn't see the aftereffects. My wife vomited all over the floor and shook for another half hour afterwards. I cleaned up the mess and then held her until she stopped trembling.

That was the night I redefined soul mate. When she finally looked at me, I expected the pity-look, not one that seared her farther into my soul. Pity didn't exist in her gaze. Horror did, but it was overridden by awe along with the depth of her love, and I actually felt our connection grow.

To me, a soul mate is someone who sees your scars and doesn't run away screaming.

The two of us were damaged in inconceivable ways, but together, we made a hell of a team. And right now, all I wanted to do was make love to my wife until the sun rose. I swept her up in my arms and marched to the other side of the house, intending to make tonight last.

Chapter 6

WHEN MORNING ROLLED AROUND, I was ready to focus on the case O'Keefe had handed us, and I waited on the deck with my coffee, enjoying the sunrise and the quiet of the morning before either Raven or Hannah woke.

A hand pounded on the glass behind me, and I turned, sending a smile to my daughter on the other side. I reached and slid the glass open.

"You didn't wake your mother, did you?" I signed, and she shook her head. "Good. She needs a little more rest."

"Okay," Hannah said, and hopped up in my lap. "Can you make me pancakes?"

I made the hand signal for yes and followed her into the kitchen. She sat at the table singing silly tunes while I whipped up a batch for us.

"Syrup or strawberries?" I asked, after I had a neat stack on a plate.

"Nutella," she said, and I laughed, shaking my head. I knew better. I had done that once, and it wound her up like an unstoppable mini-tornado. Pancakes were enough of a sugar fix without chocolate and hazelnut mixed in.

She pouted, and I held up her choices, putting them on the table with a bang to capture her attention.

"Which one?" I signed and pointed.

She crossed her arms and gave me the death ray look.

"I'm not giving you Nutella for breakfast," I signed, and collected three plates and silverware before sitting down next to her.

"Mommy lets me," she said, and I laughed, shaking my head.

"Oh, no she doesn't."

Hannah often tried to pit one of us against the other like this, and I could always read it. Raven sometimes doubted herself, but I had the inside track to know whether it was a fabrication done to get her way or a true statement. More often than not, it was a way for her to get exactly what she wanted, but she was learning.

I pointed at her and raised my eyebrows. No words were passed, but she dipped her head and mumbled, "Strawberries."

Raven shuffled into the kitchen and took a seat. Without a word, she grabbed for a plate, and I got up, fixing her coffee, because Raven didn't seem to speak in the morning without a little caffeine in her. It was more a series of grunts and adorable as hell.

I pushed her a coffee, and she acknowledged me with a nod and a smile, which is more than I usually get in the morning, and I smiled back, sending a wink in her direction.

That fine pink hue gathered in her cheeks at the same moment my phone buzzed. I dug it from my pocket and glanced at the text.

"Damian's on his way," I signed. "We need to head to the police station and talk with O'Keefe."

Her morning glow faded. "Why?" she asked; but it really was a 'what did you do now' question.

"He asked for some help on a case," I signed, and shrugged. I didn't want to get into it with Hannah within earshot, so I stood, clearing my plate. "I'll get this when I get home," I signed, and then waved at the mess in the sink.

With a peck on her cheek, I went out front to wait for Damian. I didn't want either Raven or Hannah overhearing the conversation, especially if Damian had had a bad morning. The foul look on Damian's face when he pulled into the driveway confirmed my actions.

He waited until I sat and clipped the seatbelt to toss me a notebook.

I sent him a raised eyebrow in response.

"CJ wrote everything he could remember, and I've put a check next to all those who have died in the last year." He glanced in my direction. "From what I could uncover on the web, it sounds like they all died in the same manner, too."

I stared at him and then flipped open the book. Names filled half the pages, along with their location: city, and either state or country to go along with it. I couldn't help but be impressed by the magnitude of offspring. I tapped on the single letter at the end of each line.

Damian glanced at where I tapped before refocusing on the road. "Michael, Raphael, Uriel," he said. "It doesn't contain Lucifer's bloodline."

"How long did it take him to write these?" I asked, transmitting the words in my head as I flipped page after page.

"Most of the night. I felt really shitty asking him to do it when he'd had so little sleep, but he didn't seem to mind, and he didn't ask me any questions. I think the exhaustion of a newborn has him a bit overwhelmed."

I couldn't help the grin. If anyone knew more about being overwhelmed with newborns, it was Damian. After all, he had triplets, and while we were around to help in the beginning, it was still too much to take at times. I had to hand it to his wife, though; she never looked frazzled the way Damian sometimes got.

Damian raised an eyebrow in my direction. "I do not get frazzled," he said and the irritation visible in his features echoed in his terse tone.

I responded with a loud guffaw and signed, "Bullshit," calling him out on the lie.

His eyes rolled as he pulled into the York police station.

"I would leave that in the car," he said, pointing to the notebook in my hand.

I met his gaze and debated. If we had a clue of who the next victim was, we had an obligation to let the cops in on it.

"Was there anyone killed who wasn't on this list?" I asked, signing and projecting the thought at the same time.

He shook his head, and I dropped my gaze to the scribbled names, wondering if I could trust O'Keefe with this type of information. The fact he came to us for help drew my conclusion, and before Damian could snatch the notebook from my hand, I closed it and stepped out of the car with both the notebook and the folder O'Keefe had given me at the hospital in my tight grip.

"Are you insane?" Damian hissed as he got out of the car.

I glanced over the roof and closed the car door. "If we have information that could prevent the next death, I'm not keeping it under wraps."

"That list could implicate CJ."

I hesitated, torn between doing what's right and the need to keep my brother safe. He'd be pissed if he was hauled in, but if we withheld the information, we could be considered accessories to murder, or charged with obstruction of justice at the very least. I met Damian's gaze. "It also could stop the killer."

"How are you going to explain the list?"

I shrugged. I wasn't sure O'Keefe would buy any of it, but I had to try. "Call Steve," I added, before I stepped toward the station. "O'Keefe will believe him."

Damian scoffed but flipped open his phone. I didn't wait for the conversation; instead, I headed inside. At the desk, I scribbled Captain O'Keefe on a piece of paper and cleared my throat, capturing the receptionist's attention before handing my scribbled note to her.

Her brow creased, and I sent a smile meant to dazzle and disarm. When the color rose in her cheeks, I felt the smile turn into a grin.

"Who may I tell the Captain is waiting for him?" she asked in that come-hither purr I was used to from the girls in high school.

I scribbled my name and handed it to her before signing it to convey that I couldn't speak.

Her smile dropped a notch when she realized I was handicapped and that pity-look I hated crossed her face as she picked up the phone. She swiveled so I couldn't see her lips, but when the other end was picked up, she told whomever she was talking to that she needed to come pick me up, if only to see what a freaking delicious specimen I was.

I pressed my lips together against the grin that surfaced. It had been a while since I had someone drool over me, other than my wife, and as much as I was telling myself to ignore it, it was a much-needed stroke to the ego. It was good to know I still had the same charismatic effect I snagged my wife with back in high school.

She glanced back at me with a smile and told the woman on the other end to hurry.

The hinge of the front door squeaked as it opened, and I glanced over my shoulder at Damian. He accurately read the amusement in my eyes and focused his attention on the receptionist.

"You know he can hear, right?" he asked, as he hooked his thumb in my direction.

Her gaze snapped in my direction, and her mouth dropped open seconds before her entire face bloomed red. I shrugged and sent a wink in her direction.

The door shutting off the station to the public opened, and a blonde leaned against the doorjamb. She let out a bark of a laugh.

"Well, well, well, if it isn't Tommy Ryan."

I pressed my lips together, offering a ghost of a smile before I slid my gaze to Damian before returning my attention to the blonde. For the life of me, I couldn't recall her name, but I know I slept with her during my slut days in high school.

"You still shacking up with that red-headed freak?" She batted her eyes in my direction.

My smile vanished. I lifted my left hand and pointed to my wedding band. Everyone at our high school had treated Raven like a leper, and the derogatory reference was enough to set my blood on a low boil.

"Too bad," she said, looking me up and down before swinging the door wide. "Captain O'Keefe is expecting you," she added, and waved us inside.

I walked past her, ignoring the lewd memories parading through her head, and focused on the office across the floor where Captain O'Keefe stood waiting for us.

"Thank you, Bridget," he said to her, as she took a seat outside his office.

"Since when do you hire civilians?" I signed and projected the thought.

O'Keefe glanced at me. "She's my niece," he said, like that explained it all. "She needed some income, and I needed a hand." He gave me a shrug and waved towards the chairs.

"I'm Damian Andreas," Damian said, introducing himself after giving me a sideways look when he realized I had projected my thoughts. They shook hands, and I took a seat with the folder and the notebook still in my hands.

I had no idea what I was going to say, and the silence in the room weighed on me as Damian took a seat. I looked up, meeting Captain O'Keefe's gaze as he took the chair behind his desk.

"What's on your mind?" he asked, the question directed at me.

I tossed the notebook on the desk. "This may be a comprehensive hit list."

Damian sucked in his breath and glared at me.

Captain O'Keefe flipped through the pages, and when he got to the names in the file I still had in my hands, his gaze shot up to me. "Where did you get this?"

"It's not as simple as that," I said, stalling on pushing CJ under the bus.

"Then what the hell is this?" he asked, still fanning through the book.

I traded a glance with Damian, and he crossed his arms and his eyebrow rose in a silent challenge to explain.

O'Keefe stopped on a page and pointed. "Your name is in here," he said. "So are your brother and his wife."

I nodded and started the slow explanation with my hands.

"You know I can't read sign language," he snapped, leaning forward.

I closed my eyes and sighed. "It's a list of angel bloodlines." I transmitted the thought, and the absolute silence pulled my eyelids open.

He just stared at me. Damian shifted in the seat next to me and covered his smirk.

O'Keefe cleared his throat. "Where did you get this?"

"I asked CJ to write what he remembered when..." Damian started, and trailed off, unable or unwilling to express the thought.

"Are you fucking kidding me?" O'Keefe's voice cracked, and he blinked, his gaze jumping between the two of us. "Do you think I'm an idiot?"

I put my hand up, stopping his winding fury. "Regardless of where the list came from or how it was retrieved, we found more deaths that match the ones in Portland, and they're all names on this list. The next death is written in those pages," I said in both sign language and thought transmission. "And, as I said at the hospital, it's not what you're thinking this is. A vampire doesn't just have sharp canines like in the movies; their entire mouth is full of razor-sharp teeth, like a fucking shark." His face paled at my words. "I think it's a human with the same list that CJ wrote for us last night. And the killer is systematically murdering angelic bloodlines."

"What the fuck are you talking about?" O'Keefe's face reddened.

"Archangels," Damian said, pulling the captain's attention his way. "A very long time ago, they interacted with humans, and that is a list of the living descendants."

O'Keefe barked a laugh and leaned back in the chair.

A knock on the door interrupted him before he could continue.

"Come in," he snapped, and I didn't need to turn when the door opened.

"Morning, Jim," Steve said, as he stepped into the room and closed the door behind him. "Damian thought I might be of some help."

He laughed and pointed at the two of us. "Do you know what kind of bullshit they were trying to feed me?"

Steve let out a soft laugh and walked past O'Keefe to the window. "What exactly did my son tell you?" he asked, sending a sideways glance in my direction.

"He said the killer is murdering angel descendants." O'Keefe didn't mince words, going straight to the entire point of the notebook.

Steve turned towards me and raised his eyebrows. "Where did you come up with that?"

I pointed to the notebook that O'Keefe was still leafing through.

"CJ wrote what he remembered of the wall of ancestors," Damian said, and Steve's gaze moved to him. "I recognized one name, and on a hunch asked CJ to write what he could."

"And?"

"And everyone in the file the Captain gave us is on that list."

Steve sighed and turned his attention back to Captain O'Keefe.

O'Keefe met his stare and blew out an exhale before leaning back in his seat. "So, this shit is real." It wasn't phrased as a question.

"Afraid so," Steve said.

"The captain came to us because he suspected it might be a vampire," I signed, and then handed him the file. When Steve flipped it open to the first picture, he let out a small laugh and closed the file, handing it back.

"That's not what a vampire bite looks like." He rolled up his sleeve and turned his forearm in O'Keefe's direction. The scar remained from the bite he'd received while guarding Valerie. If Naomi hadn't been quick to respond, Steve would have died.

O'Keefe looked at the jagged scar and winced.

"If Damian's wife hadn't sucked the poison out, I would have died." He offered the slightest of smiles when O'Keefe slumped in the chair. "I was just as freaked out as you are to find out there are things out there that are much worse than the Windwalker."

O'Keefe stared at him for longer than he should have, his brain swirling in an almost unreadable pattern, as if the facts were short-circuiting him. He dropped his gaze to the notebook and turned page after page, scanning the names slowly before he finally looked up at me.

"Angels are real?" he asked in a small voice, like a child finding wonder.

"So are demons," I signed and transmitted at the same time.

He blinked rapidly and then stared down at the words like they would change, like this conversation was part of an elaborate dream he would wake from any minute.

"Why would someone want angel blood?" he asked, and a chill ran though me. I glanced at Steve and his face paled as much as Damian's next to me. None of us had considered that, and we all moved our gazes back to the captain at the same time.

Captain O'Keefe's mind worked the same way Steve's did, and that is why Steve had been such a great FBI agent. Although he attempted to attribute it to Jennifer's clairvoyance, it really was his base instinct to break something down to its simplest form.

"To regenerate," Damian said very softly.

O'Keefe raised his gaze. "Excuse me?"

We all remained silent as the horror of the details sank in. Not only was the assassin killing angel-kin, but he was also draining them of blood. And if this was Lucifer's hit list, it would only make sense that the killer was shipping the blood instead of doing God knows what with it.

"Holy shit," Steve finally muttered, and took a seat on the old leather couch by the door. He ran his hands through his hair and stared at the floor.

We hadn't heard from Lucifer since we rescued our father and closed the portal in Canada. The quiet had been very nice for a change and I think we all just wrote him off. But the fact there still were portals we hadn't closed remained a dark stain on all our future plans. If we were right about this, that would mean considerable opposition. Especially if Lucifer was able to power up before CJ took another run at him.

"Both your sons are on this list," O'Keefe added, and Steve met his gaze with a nod.

"I'm well aware of my family's heritage," he said softly, and glanced in my direction, meeting my questioning stare.

Pages rustled as O'Keefe flipped back and forth, scanning the names. His mind wrestled with the facts we'd dumped on him, unsure of whether or not to believe us. He wasn't as stubborn as he once had been, and with Steve's acceptance of what had been revealed, he was doubting his beliefs, or lack thereof.

"So, there's a heaven?" he asked timidly, and glanced up.

I had CJ's memories, and I gave a nod, confirming the question, and the captain's eyes narrowed.

"How the hell can you know that?" His voice carried the incredulous expression carved into his features.

"Because CJ was there," I signed, and Steve translated even before I finished. "It's a long story," I added with a shrug.

"What about hell?" he asked, crossing his arms as skepticism layered over his doubts.

I nodded again, but this time without adding any explanation. CJ's memories of the portals made me shiver in the seat, and our father in hellhound form brought forth a rash of gooseflesh across my arms. My jaw involuntarily clenched as I dropped my eyes to the floor, studying the industrial carpeting.

"I'm not sure what to believe," O'Keefe said, and papers shuffled again. "But let's just say I bought all this shit you are shoveling in my direction," O'Keefe added, focusing on me. "Who do you think is next?" He turned the notebook back in my direction and slid it across the desk.

"Do you have a map of Maine?" I asked, and he nodded, pulling one out of his drawer. He spread it out over his desk and Damian and I plotted the deaths on the map, starting with the ones Damian had discovered in northern Maine, using the dates and times to show the progression. Clusters of small x's showed the path of the killer from Caribou, Maine, all the way down to Portland.

He stepped around as I pulled out the notebook and marked the remaining names in the Portland area. Thankfully, there were only two left in Portland. The next cluster was in York, with only one other between our little family band and the Portland strikes.

Three more deaths before this lunatic hit us. My daughter was on this list, along with Damian's wife and kids. I traded a gaze with my business partner, and he stared at the map, formulating the same countdown in his head as I had gone through.

"Just out of curiosity, what do the single letters mean?" O'Keefe asked.

"Michael, Uriel, and Raphael," Damian said. "It denotes which bloodline the person falls under."

"What about Gabriel?" he asked mockingly.

Damian stared him down. "Gabriel only had one child."

"And how would you know that?"

The glare Damian sent in his direction chilled the room. "I know."

Captain O'Keefe chuckled like he had truly lost it. "I can't believe I haven't thrown you all in jail... or the psych ward." He kept laughing and when the door swung open with no warning, we all turned.

CJ walked in looking as ragged as I expected, but underneath the tired exterior burned an anger I recognized. My brother was pissed, and that's never a good thing. The door slammed behind him, and silence settled over the room.

"What gives you the right to share that list with anyone, let alone the cops?" he snarled at me. Captain O'Keefe stood from behind the desk, his hand automatically reaching for his sidearm in reaction to CJ's tone.

"Someone's collecting angel blood and making the cops think it's a vampire," Damian said, pulling CJ's attention. He gestured towards the map like that would explain our pulling in someone ill-equipped to tangle with the supernatural.

"I suggest you take a seat," Captain O'Keefe said, leveling a stare meant to intimidate. "Otherwise, I might be inclined to throw you in the holding tank until all this is sorted out."

CJ turned his glare in the captain's direction and his eyes narrowed in warning. "Sit your ass down," he said in that commanding tone that normal people can't resist.

O'Keefe sat, but his face registered shock at his complete inability to disregard the given order.

"That list is not for public consumption," CJ said, but his voice lost the edge it had when he first walked in.

I pointed to the map. "Look at the progression of murders. They are headed directly for us, and Valerie is on that list." I projected the thought louder than I anticipated and everyone in the room winced at the volume.

Our eyes locked and I could almost hear his thought process. If the killer found Valerie, they would also find Alex. The parental instinct kicked in and everything clicked in his overtired mind. He closed his eyes and dragged a hand down his face with a sigh. He nodded and glanced at O'Keefe.

"Captain, you are out of your element. This will put you in mortal danger."

O'Keefe actually laughed at him. "I'm a cop. This is what I signed up for."

"You're a cop in York, Maine. This isn't New York City, where you could be shot while sitting in your cruiser," CJ countered, and I covered the smirk that formed on my lips. "No disrespect," he added in a much softer voice. "But Damian and my brother are uniquely qualified to deal with this. You aren't."

"What exactly are we dealing with?" O'Keefe asked, moving his gaze from CJ to me before landing on Steve. No one spoke and O'Keefe scanned us all again.

"I have to go," CJ said, and I gave him a nod. Within a blink, the space he occupied vacated, and the sudden disappearance of my brother silenced whatever O'Keefe was about to say.

"What the fuck?"

Steve chuckled from his position on the couch. "Jim, you really don't know what you're stepping into here."

"I told you there were things much worse than vampires out there," I signed, and transmitted the thought. "I just never qualified it in a way you could understand. Think of the biggest bad and multiply it by a thousand."

He met my gaze while his brain made the connections. "If angels exist..." He trailed off and his face drained of all color. His mind combed over the entire conversation in a matter of seconds, shuffling and reshuffling all the details like a blackjack dealer. "Why would the devil need to regenerate?" he asked after a few minutes of silence.

"Because CJ nearly destroyed him," Damian said.

I guess he figured with CJ's grand exit, there was nothing left to hide.

"What?" He blinked, like someone had thrown sand in his eyes.

"There are only a few people on this earth who have danced with the devil and survived the ordeal. As circumstances would have it, they have all lived under my roof at one time or another." Steve said.

I glanced back at him, and he sat with his arms crossed, staring at O'Keefe like he'd just delivered his breakfast order instead of confirming the existence of the devil. I returned my gaze to Captain O'Keefe.

"Is he..." He pointed to where CJ had stood but I cut him off with a shake of my head.

"No. CJ isn't an angel. He's a descendant like we are." I transmitted the thought and waved my finger between Damian and me.

O'Keefe glanced at Damian and then turned the pages in the book before he glanced back up. "Any relation to Naomi, Grace, Gabriel and Michael Andreas?"

Damian nodded. "My wife and children," he said.

O'Keefe glanced at the names again. "You aren't listed in this book."

Damian huffed a laugh. "That's because I'm Gabriel's son."

O'Keefe stared at him. "You are an offspring of an archangel?" His voice cracked and his eyebrows arched. He slowly stood and turned, looking out his window, processing everything. "Then what is he. No human can just disappear like that." He snapped his fingers and turned back to us.

"He... inherited my ability to be in two places at once," Steve said from the couch.

O'Keefe pointed at him. "You never explained that shit to me."

Steve cracked a smile. "You never offered to buy me a drink."

O'Keefe muttered under his breath, but kept eye contact. "So, what are you?"

"An ex-FBI agent who inherited more than just money from Ty Ryan and his wife."

"Who, I am assuming, were also descendants?"

"Yup."

"So, does being an angel descendant warrant..." he waved towards the empty space and then pointed at me. "Or mind reading and thought projecting like him?"

Steve sighed and shrugged.

"No." Damian said. "None of the descendants I've ever come across had any discernible level of extra sensory perception like these boys do." He pointed at me. "They seem to be unique in that manner."

"And how many 'descendants' have you been in contact with," O'Keefe said, with a voice so filled with sarcasm that I let out a huff, catching it before it became an all-out laugh.

Damian leaned forward with his eyes narrowed. "Twenty-five-hundred-year's worth." He settled back in the seat. "More or less," he added with a smugness that would have made me grit my teeth had I not been so stunned by his honesty.

Oh fuck. The thought slammed home and my jaw loosened as I stared at Damian, wondering what the hell he was thinking. He sent a glare in my direction and focused back on the captain.

O'Keefe's eyelids were fluttering like hummingbird wings while his mind short-circuited. Even Steve huffed a laugh of disbelief. Damian really shit the bed with this one and I knew what was coming before O'Keefe blew sky high.

"What. The. Fuck." O'Keefe's baritone voice blared at us. If this had been a cartoon, it would have tipped us all over like a gale force wind.

The door opened and what's her name poked her head inside. "Is everything all right?"

O'Keefe recovered faster than I expected, and his gaze snapped to hers. "Yes. Now close the damned door."

Her eyes widened just before the door clicked shut, and I glanced back at O'Keefe.

"I think it's time for you to leave," O'Keefe growled low, and I sighed, standing up with no intention of leaving. I made the come here gesture, and he glared at me.

"Just come here," I said in my head and he paused but stepped closer.

I had never shared anyone's memories but my own before, and I wasn't sure how this worked, but I inhaled and concentrated on locking the power behind the door so none of it leaked out. It was hard enough for me to deal with; I'm not sure what it would do to O'Keefe if he got some residual supercharge. Once I was sure I wouldn't transfer any of CJ's mojo, I focused on only Damian's memories and reached out, placing the palm of my hand on his forehead. I held his gaze and sent as much of the memories swarming in my head as I dared.

His breathing became ragged, and his eyes glossed over. Sweat broke out under my palm and when he blinked and his eyes refocused on mine, I pulled my hand away and took a seat. Captain O'Keefe slowly dropped into his chair.

His pallid color told me enough, but then his gaze moved beyond me to Steve, and finally settled on Damian. He blinked a few times and licked his lips.

"You were a... a..." He cleared his throat again. "A vampire?"

"Yes."

O'Keefe wiped his face. "And Lucifer?" he asked without finishing, shuddering at the vision of Lucifer destroying all Damian held dear.

"He's a joy, isn't he?"

O'Keefe let out a high-pitched laugh and his gaze landed on Steve again.

"Mind. Blown," he said, staring behind me.

Steve chuckled. "Yeah, I went the denial route at first, myself. But then, seeing the bloodsuckers firsthand, well, that seemed to change my entire perspective. And Lucifer is the most terrifying thing I've ever come up against."

His eyes widened.

"Show him, Tom," Steve said, and I glanced behind me, shaking my head.

O'Keefe saved me the pain by clearing his throat. "I've seen enough," he whispered.

Steve let out a laugh and met his gaze. "Do you want to solve the only open case this town has?"

O'Keefe's incessant blinking was back, and his jaw slowly dropped so that his mouth formed a small 'o'.

"Of course, you wouldn't be able to formally close the case," he added and crossed his arms. "But at least you'd know what happened."

"Are you trying to get arrested?" I signed in his direction, and he glared at me for a moment before nodding his head toward the captain.

"Show him what happened the day Damian's triplets were born," he ordered.

Chapter 7

I GROUND MY JAW tight, turning back to Captain O'Keefe. The blinking had stopped, and he moved his gaze to mine with a quick nod.

I knew better. Nothing could prepare him for the hell he was about to see.

I wondered how wise this was as I zeroed in on that night. The horror of it all, from the battle in the cove to the bloodshed over the snow-covered lawn.

Damian wouldn't look at me. Instead, his eyes remained glued to something beyond the window. That night signaled a change for all of us. It opened the doors to where we were now, and he blamed himself for bringing all this shit on us.

I sighed and stood.

Captain O'Keefe leaned forward in the chair, and I had a moment to be thankful he was sitting because this vision was my viewpoint, not Damian's, and it would come with the raw emotion surrounding the entire event.

I knew where to start and I knew where to end, but that didn't make it any easier to pull the memory out of the box.

"I can handle it," O'Keefe said, and I met his gaze.

"Yeah, but I'm not sure I can," I transmitted, and steadied my breathing.

When my palm touched his forehead, the entire ordeal roared back.

STEVE GUIDED US ACROSS the snow-covered lawn toward Paradise cove. CJ and I followed the group, and every muscle in my body wound tight. This was as bad as the anticipation of the psycho's knife. I wasn't sure if we would walk out of this, even with my brother's incredible power, and all I wanted to do was hold Raven tight and protect her from harm. CJ

glanced at me, and I gave him a slight nod. He could feel my apprehension as we crossed onto the narrow path leading to the cove.

"This is the perfect place for an ambush," Damian muttered while glancing at the proximity of the tree lines on both sides. My eyes darted to the dark woods as well.

"You'll be okay," CJ said, his voice soft, falling with the wind surrounding us as he traded a glance with me. I noticed the lack of the usual 'I promise', which was my first sign that my brother was just as freaked out as I was.

We made it to the glen without incident and Steve threw Damian a canister of salt.

"Make yourself useful," he said, and Damian raised an eyebrow.

"Salt?"

"Yes, make a barrier at the wood line."

"I'm not sure this is going to work," he said, but stepped to the path we'd just crossed over. He poured a thick line across the snow-covered ground, continuing onto the frozen water of the cove.

"Now what?" he asked.

Steve traded a glance with Jennifer and then started clearing a space with his feet. "Now we make a fire and wait," Steve said. CJ and I helped clear the snow off with our feet, revealing the deep green moss covering the land mass.

"You know, for such a brilliant investigator, you can be a complete idiot," Damian said, and Steve looked up at him with a crease of confusion between his eyes. "Step aside."

Damian crossed to a spot just inside the salt line. It took a moment, and then the snow rolled away like an old carpet clearing the moss and the ice all the way to the far edge of the cove where the lake began in earnest.

I was impressed and CJ rolled his eyes, but Steve was pissed, and he just crossed his arms, sending a glare at Damian in that way that made me uncomfortable. CJ smirked and turned away, like a laugh would just cause more tension.

"What? You've got the power to do this. Why the hell would you do it manually?"

"Because it reminds me I'm human, and not some all-powerful god," Steve answered, his tone as sharp as his gaze. I stepped closer to Raven in response, our hands intertwining, and she gave me a quick squeeze.

"You really know how to get under his skin," I said, and Damian's head snapped in my direction. My voice was completely restored, as it always was when I stepped into this cove. I sent a sliver of a smile at his wide-eyed stare.

Before he commented, he was yanked into the darkness, and just like that, Naomi snapped into tiger form. Instinct took over, and I let go of Raven's hand, pushing both her and Jennifer behind me. I know I wasn't super charged like CJ, Steve, and Damian, but I could put up a hell of a fight. I pulled the gun out of my pocket, but before I could level it at the ruckus coming towards us, CJ grabbed my arm.

"It's Damian," he said, and as soon as the words fell from his lips along with a plume of white air, Damian stepped back into the cove, visibly shaken with blood dripping from his arm.

Raven's grip on my shoulder tightened, and I looked back at her wide eyes.

"It'll be okay," I said, and her gaze moved to mine but no matter how much I wanted to promise her we'd walk out of this, I really didn't know if that was true or not. Her physical touch gave me an ounce of courage to believe in something more and I turned back towards the surrounding woods.

Light illuminated the cove, telling me enough. I knew if I turned, our father would be there. He always made the dark shine, ever since he died and took the position of Steve's guardian angel.

I kept my focus, and the barrel of the gun pointed towards the perimeter that I was covering. The woods shifted and my breath caught in my throat. Ice filled my veins at the sight of at least a dozen vampires stepping into view. The salt would do nothing to stop them and from the sudden loss of color in Damian's face, I gathered this was not a good thing.

"Jesus," Steve muttered.

The blood suckers stopped, collectively smiling, with their gazes locked on Damian.

"The great Damian Andreas," one of them growled. His voice settled over the cove like a form of Black Death, and I swallowed my fear, focusing my sights between the eyes of the nearest bastard.

"I'll give you to the count of three to leave; otherwise, you'll be burning in hell before you can blink." Damian raised his gun, pointing it towards the idiot who spoke. Naomi growled, and we all clicked off our safety, making sure we were locked and loaded and ready to spray bullets.

"Don't shoot. We're going to fry their asses," CJ's thought filled my brain, and I traded a quick glance and a nod, telling him I heard him.

"One," Damian said. The vampires laughed.

"You're going to shoot us?" the lead asshole said and chuckled. "You should know better."

Damian smiled, looking over the gun. "Two, and yes, I know better," he said, and the vampire's cocky stance waned.

"Platinum?" he gasped, and took a step back, fear transitioning his features from shadow back to pale white.

"And we're all expert shots," Damian said and didn't wait for them to attack or retreat. Instead, he yelled, "Three!"

A wave of heat rolled across the moss, rippling the air as it fanned out to encompass the mass of vampires. The stench of burned flesh filled the air, along with the dust of decimated vampires.

A shift in the wind blew the dust into the woods. When Damian turned towards the lake, his mouth dropped open. We all turned to see what had shocked him so visibly.

My father stood on the ice surrounded by a host of angels. A fucking army of angels, and I stared, *dumbfounded. The only two without wings stepped forward and Damian uttered something in a foreign language I didn't know.*

When he transitioned back to English, his words sent a shiver through me.

"Papa, is that really you?"

"Damian," he whispered. "My son," he added.

If I recall the bits of conversation from the house correctly, his father was the archangel Gabriel. I glanced at CJ, and his eyes turned to mine, like they always did when I needed clarification.

He nodded. "He hasn't seen his father since he was really little," CJ said. "His father is the Archangel Gabriel, and that's Michael standing next to him."

"No shit," I said, glancing back at the pair. Michael didn't look as formidable as our father did, and perhaps that's because he no longer had wings.

"Damian has their grace. That's why they don't have wings." CJ's narrative filled me in, and I sighed, once again the last to get all the pieces of the puzzle.

"How?" Damian asked, scanning the white-winged beings in our midst.

"The cove," I said aloud, and Damian's head snapped towards me. "It's kind of a magical place in case you haven't noticed." I gave him a shrug and Steve cleared his throat, pulling our attention to him.

"I promised you an army," Steve said, and waved his hand at the heavenly host, grinning like he knew a particularly intriguing secret.

Movement pulled my attention back to the woods, and a chill swept the area, pressing down on all of us. We moved tighter together in response to the solid line of demons that stepped into view.

The next wave of assailants took up their posts, side by side with a legion of hellhounds. Naomi actually stepped back at the numbers, and our fear blended together, leaving a metallic taste in my mouth.

Terror gripped every one of us, and we spread out on the shoreline far enough away from the woods to be safe for the moment. Steve took the left side, and Damian took the right. CJ stood dead center. Jennifer, Raven, and I stood a step behind, relying on the power centers to provide a solid wall of defense.

However, my gun was now trained on the closest demon. Steve had taught me how to shoot, and between that and my martial arts training, I was sure I could take down a few of them before they tore me to shreds. I'd kill as many as I could to protect my wife and Jennifer, and I steeled myself for battle.

The angels filtered between us, providing a protective barrier around me and the girls, and I clenched my teeth in frustration, turning towards the one that probably ordered the extra defense. My father gave me a shrug. One that said he wasn't there before, but this time, he'd make damned sure I walked out of this unharmed.

My heart scrambled in my chest, pumping a beat that nearly seized my lungs, and I traded a glance with CJ. He swallowed and curled his hands around his revolver, aiming it at the closest demon.

The air sparked with tension, and when the demons blocking the path parted, all hope for winning this battle faded. Lucifer stepped inside the ring, swiping a clean path through the salt Damian had lain down, and he wasn't alone.

He dragged Steve's partner, Sarah, forward, tossing her at his feet in front of him. When she raised her bruised face, Steve cursed under his *breath and the gun moved from the line of demons to Lucifer.*

Lucifer just grinned at the assembly and his black wings fluttered as he cracked his knuckles. His gazed moved over the crowd of angels. "What have we here?" he asked, scanning the line until his gaze landed on Gabriel and Michael. He tilted his head in contemplation, and then his gaze moved back to Steve.

"This lovely police officer was particularly useful," he said, meeting Steve's glare and waving his hand in Sarah's direction.

Her gaze bounced from the demons surrounding us to the angels in line, landing on the tiger pacing in front of me. Then they jumped back to Steve.

"What the fuck?" she whispered, and Steve offered her a half laugh.

"I told you not to go to the house," he said, and I recognized the regret in his voice. "You should have listened this time."

Lucifer grabbed a handful of her hair.

"Let go of me, asshole," Sarah snapped, swatting at his hand. While her voice was defiant and full of moxie, her eyes held a soul-crushing fear that I knew all too well. I had felt the same fear when I was

strapped to the table in Georgia; knowing death is beating down your door and there isn't a damned thing you can do about it.

He pulled her to her feet, bringing her close to him. Her elbow connected with his stomach, and he chuckled in her ear.

"I like my women feisty," he purred in her ear, keeping his gaze locked on Steve's. This was just the beginning of his dance, and we all knew Sarah was doomed.

We were all doomed.

"I'll tell you what," he said, running a sharp nail lightly down her arm. "I'll let you and your family go, along with this lovely officer, if you leave us to settle our differences." He nodded toward Naomi and Damian, negotiating a deal that would seal Damian in his grave.

I knew a lie when I heard one and that one was a doozie. One glance at his arsenal and I knew if we stepped out of the cove, we were all dead. I didn't need the infusion of Damian's memories, like Steve and CJ had, to feel the evil radiating from this bastard.

"That includes leaving the angel and his son," Lucifer clarified, his gaze landing on my father, narrowing into a hateful expression.

What the fuck does this bastard want with my brother? The thought barreled through my mind and I saw CJ tense, and he glanced over his shoulder at me. Just the look alone was enough. I didn't need his added 'Just chill,' but it pinged in my mind just the same.

Steve's jaw clenched, and his gaze dropped to Sarah.

"Do your magic and get me out of this," Sarah said. The panic reached her voice as Steve's head shook back and forth.

His entire being shook, and the frustration and anger pulsing in his veins drifted over me.

"You bastard," Damian whispered, and Lucifer sent a chilling smile in his direction.

"I can't do that," Steve said, and Damian glanced at him. Jennifer breeched the line of angels and laid her hand on his shoulder in a show of solidarity. She gave him strength to do what was necessary, even with the silent sobs shaking her form.

Lucifer's hand ripped Sarah's shirt open, revealing a modest sports bra, and he tilted his *head, smiling as his fingernails dimpled the skin over her heart. "Last chance," he said.*

"I'm sorry, Sarah," Steve said, his eyes filled with tears and his lips pressed together.

Sarah's scream shattered the night, followed by the report of a gun. A ringing silence encompassed us. Smoke drifted from the end of Steve's revolver, and I stared at where his bullet landed.

Lucifer's fingers were buried knuckle deep in Sarah's chest, but that's not what silenced her scream. The neat bullet hole between her eyes had sent her to heaven before Lucifer could rip her heart out.

I knew what that shot would do to Steve. But he chose a more humane death for his partner; though his logical mind wouldn't be able to bury the guilt, despite being the right move. If he hadn't ended her life, Lucifer would have made her suffering last as long as possible.

He lowered his arms, and his chin dropped to his chest. His breath hitched once. With a violent shake of his head, his tear-stained glare landed on Lucifer and the gun rose back in place.

"Get the fuck off my property," he said with a growl.

"As soon as I have my whore," he said.

Steve pulled the trigger again, but this time nothing happened until he moved the aim to the demon closest to Lucifer and then the gun jumped to life, expelling another round. The shot was as true as the one that took Sarah's life, and the first demon fell.

Lucifer yanked his hand from Sarah's flesh and tossed her next to the dead demon. He licked his fingers and scowled, glaring at Steve. The minute he stepped forward, my father interceded, blocking the devil's path.

That hateful glare reappeared and Lucifer snapped his fingers, Christopher Ryan appeared in the center of the clearing, bleeding and on his knees, his screams filling the silent woods, echoing on the dark lake as the hellhounds tasked with ripping him to shreds continued their attack.

This time, my father moved; his face filled with a wrath I had never seen before, and CJ took a step toward him. Before I could stop him, both Steve and Damian took hold of his arms, keeping him from entering the violent scene in front of us. This was just a primer to the bigger war, one meant as an appetizer to drive the hounds in line into a frenzy, preparing them for attack.

"You can't stop it," Damian said when CJ tried to rip out of his grasp.

He turned a pleading gaze in his direction when the first hellhound turned on our dad.

A flare of satisfaction bloomed in me when my father ripped the hellhound in two with his bare hands, and from the expression on Lucifer's face, he didn't expect that at all.

My dad kicked ass.

My father grabbed Chris around the waist and launched toward the heavens, pulling his brother out of range of the hellhounds into the single beacon of light, disappearing from view before Lucifer could yank him back to the earth.

Lucifer's furious gaze dropped from the sky to Damian, then moved to CJ. His face crinkled and he roared his aggravation, squeezing a fist in front of him. Damian stepped into Lucifer's line of sight, and nothing happened at first. Then, out of nowhere, three of the demons next to Lucifer burst, exploding into neat balls of flame.

The surprise of the back-to-back events stunned everyone, and nothing moved until a streak of *lightning flared and my father landed on one knee in the center of the clearing like Thor arriving for battle. His wings smoldered, sending tendrils of smoke into the air, but when he lifted his head, his fury filled the space and he stood, shifting into a battle stance.*

"You've cheated me for the last time," Lucifer growled and pointed at my dad.

"Game on, you bastard," he said, and leveled the glare I had seen when I was little. The one that dubbed the man the Angel of Death while he was alive. And it evoked a tremor, a chill that bit at my heels and spread like a four-alarm fire. As much as I loved my father, he could scare the living crap out of me with that look.

Naomi hissed behind me, and the spell that held us in place broke. Damian aimed his gun at the closest hellhound and squeezed the trigger. The report of gunfire shattered the stillness, breaking the stalemate between good and evil.

Thirty demons went down in the span of the ten seconds it took the four of us to empty our clips and the only one who took the time to re-load was me. The angels charged forward, meeting the advancing demons in the center, but Steve, CJ, and Damian stayed put, protecting us.

When I stepped between CJ and Damian, leveling the gun at the melee, Damian pushed my hand down and shook his head.

"Hold on to those. We might need them," he said, meeting my gaze and pushing me back into the safety of the cocoon they'd created. I felt completely useless and frustrated, and Raven gripped my arm, her attention focused on the bloodbath in front of us.

"On three," CJ said. "One," he breathed low, his voice almost lost over the bellows of fighting angels and demons.

The charge built in the air, and I pulled Jennifer and Raven closer to me, taking a step back to give the three of them more room to execute whatever they were planning.

"Two," Damian said.

"Three!" Steve yelled.

The air rippled like a wave rolling across the field, leaving only a bloody mist in its wake, along with four stunned angels.

My father glanced at us with a maniacal grin.

Lucifer stood at the edge of the field, scanning the gory remains of his army.

Michael and Gabriel stared at the mess with open mouths.

Only the sound of blood rain filled the space, and I realize the three of them had annihilated demons and angels alike. Only archangels remained, and my gaze landed on my father. A shiver caught my soul, turning my blood as cold as the frigid water behind me.

We moved closer to my dad. Michael and Gabriel squared up to Lucifer, but he wasn't done with his arsenal of tricks.

Naomi howled, and I blinked down at the writhing cat before my gaze jumped back to Lucifer.

Damian charged without thought, and got one hit in before Lucifer's backhand hit him, spinning him onto the ground. The howl turned into an ear-piercing scream, snapping my gaze to Naomi. She lay in a ball, in human form, holding her stomach, screaming in pain.

The black power moved from Naomi to CJ, dropping him to his knees as he held his chest. His head dipped and his hands balled into fists. I went to take a step to help him, but both Jennifer and Raven held onto me, their fright keeping me in place. CJ was in pain and my stomach writhed. The muscles in his arms stood out under the coat, tensing against whatever assault Lucifer was sending his way. When he snapped his gaze from the ground back at Lucifer, the devil stumbled back, nearly falling on his ass.

CJ stood, with his breath coming in shallow bursts from the exertion, and he ignored everyone, focusing his attention on the devil, now engaged in a fight to the death with both Michael and Gabriel.

Damian scrambled to Naomi, and his frantic eyes searched her face before looking up at Raven and me. He glanced to where Steve stood, splitting his attention between the fight and us. Naomi's paleness caught his attention, and he stepped closer just as Damian whispered, "Can you fix her?"

Steve bent down and delivered a kiss to Naomi's forehead and light danced over her form, rejuvenating her body, filling her hollow cheeks with a healthy glow. She blinked at him and then her eyes rolled back and she went limp.

"What did you do?" Damian asked, alarmed by her slip into unconsciousness.

"She'll be fine," Raven said, "But we need to get her out of here," she added, watching the movement of the three archangels. "The path isn't blocked anymore," she said, pointing.

Damian didn't hesitate. He picked Naomi up and headed for the open escape, and we followed him at an all-out sprint. We burst into the house and Damian placed Naomi on the couch, pushing her hair away from her face.

"Come on, baby," he whispered, pressing his lips to hers. She didn't respond, and he turned toward us, his eyes begging for help. We all knew the healing power tends to knock people out, but he didn't. Even so, the lack of concern on our parts seemed to calm him.

Raven stepped forward, her gaze averted, but she forced eye contact. "She'll be okay; her life force is still strong." She touched his cheek. "Your babies shine just like you."

"Jesus," Steve's mutter called our attention away from Naomi and out the window. Lucifer stalked onto the property. The severed heads of Gabriel and Michael dangled from each of his hands, and he held them up for us to see. His roar of triumph left me shaking, and I gulped down the fear.

"Shit," my father's voice rang out behind us, and we turned, staring down the only other angel standing.

Damian pointed to Naomi. "Keep her safe. That's all I ask," he said, moving his gaze across our faces, and then he turned and crossed to the door.

"What do you think you're doing?" Steve asked.

"Ending this," Damian said and stepped outside.

My father sighed and glanced at us, his gaze moving from mine to CJ's, and then he glanced at Steve. "You know I can't just let him go after the devil alone," he said.

We all nodded, and he paused, giving us a nod before turning and following Damian out into the battle zone.

I stared out the window with CJ by my side. Words passed and then Lucifer belted out a laugh that rattled the windowpane. He leaned back, cackling at the sky. My father launched, leaving Damian standing in place like a shocked little kid.

The battle between my father and Lucifer raged, dredging up a white flurry around the two angels. My heartbeat rammed my throat, drawing my breath in fast pants of anxiety that matched CJ's. Raven slid a swaddled baby into my arms without so much as a glance outside and I held the infant tight, mindful of not crushing him.

Red splattered white, and CJ bellowed at the vision of our father's head in the demon's grip. His palms banged against the cold windowpane as blood rained down on my father's wings. My mind flashed back to my mother's head propped up on the end of the surgical table, her dead eyes staring at me the way my father's were now.

I glanced down at the small package in my arms, looking for something to erase the visions assaulting me; the boy momentarily distracted me from the darkness bathing my heart. When I returned my gaze out the window, the scene swarmed through a mist of tears. My heart squeezed against the devastation.

The baby in my arms represented hope, but how could a mere mortal take on the devil and win when archangels fell? When my father fell? I hitched a breath, pressing my lips together.

The child tempered my reaction and the cry of disdain coming from the baby's lips pulled both our eyes to the swaddled bundle; Damian's firstborn, and I propped him up on my shoulder, gently bouncing to ease his pain.

When I returned my gaze outside, Damian's hand shot toward Lucifer's chest. I had no clue what to expect, but when Damian's hand came into view, holding a beating heart, my eyes widened in shock.

And then Damian did the unthinkable: he took a bite of the bloody muscle.

I shivered with disgust; it burned through the horror of all the destruction that occurred tonight, and I covered my mouth with my free hand. One look at CJ told me he felt the same burn roiling in my stomach.

The moment the last piece of Lucifer's heart disappeared into Damian's mouth, the heavens opened, and a blinding light encompassed him, dropping Damian to his knees. I stared at the man in the midst of the heavenly glow, wondering if the angel grace effect would last. CJ and I traded a glance before refocusing on the bloodied winter scene. The glow faded, and Damian climbed to his feet. The fury etched into his features made me want to shrink away from the glass. I've only seen that kind of wrath once, and it was painted on my father's face.

A blast leaped from Damian, enveloping Lucifer, leaving only torched earth where the devil had stood. I gaped, blinking rapidly, trying to make sense of what had just happened.

I PULLED MY HAND away from Captain O'Keefe's forehead and took a seat. The lump in my throat matched the wobbly vision, and I blinked, sending hot paths down my cheeks. I had buried that scene away since it happened, and reliving it was just as painful as it had been that night. I stared at the ground, feeling more like the scared seventeen-year-old the captain hauled into the police station years ago, as opposed to the man I was today.

A hand landed on my shoulder, and I glanced back at Steve as he gave me a squeeze of support. I didn't want to glare, but it was already forming. Reliving that shit opened wounds that had partially healed. Now they were raw enough to evoke the emotions again.

I turned towards the captain, trying to scrape off the horror tightening my throat, and what met my gaze softened the swirl in my stomach and made me press my lips together against a smirk.

The man trembled in the chair, just staring at a spot on his desk. Blotchy red stained his cheeks, standing out in stark relief against the pasty white of his skin. He finally raised his gaze to mine and opened his mouth to speak, but only a wheeze came out.

"Breathe, Captain," I whispered in my mind, giving him a nod of encouragement.

He took a large inhale through his nose and let it out of his mouth, repeating until it didn't sound like the startup of a motorcycle.

"Holy shit," he finally muttered. He blinked a few more times and let out a shaky laugh. "I take it back. I don't want to know this shit exists," he said, drawing smiles to all our faces. His expression sobered as his gaze landed on Steve. "I don't know if I could have made the same call," he said, his voice a fraction stronger.

Steve remained quiet, and I didn't need to turn and look to know he was staring at his hands. His mind was already reviewing that same night, looking for an alternative that wouldn't have left Sarah dead, and he couldn't find a palatable solution beyond what he did. His sigh signaled the end of his memory inspection.

"I couldn't..." he started and stopped.

Captain O'Keefe raised his hand to stop Steve. "Just tell me where her remains are," he said a little more forcefully.

I glanced back at Steve as he finished his shrug in response.

O'Keefe raised his eyebrows. "Cat got your tongue?"

"The place was clean when we went back after taking Naomi to the hospital. No evidence that there had been a bloodbath exists. The only sign that any of it really happened was the scorched grass. Everything else was as pristine as when we arrived."

"You have got to be joking," O'Keefe said. "How do you even know she's dead?"

I didn't wait for prompting; I reached out and slammed my palm on his forehead, transmitting one of CJ's memories. The one that not only proved Sarah was dead but also proved there was indeed a heaven, and it really wasn't anything we envisioned.

It only took seconds and then I leaned back, crossing my arms, waiting for him to draw the conclusion. His gaze snapped to the empty space where CJ had stood earlier and then back to me as he muddled through the memory.

"He... died?"

"Not exactly," I signed and both Damian and Steve translated aloud. "But that's not my story to tell," I added, this time following it with the mind transmission.

O'Keefe's gaze moved from mine to Damian's as the memory transfer fully hit. "Your wife turns into a tiger?" he asked, blinking again at the delayed reaction of all the facts.

Damian let out a huff of a laugh. "Yes. She does that whenever demons are near."

O'Keefe studied us and then turned to me.

"Is that what attacked Raven's father?"

I nodded, keeping his gaze.

"Jesus," he whispered and rubbed his face. The ramifications of all we could do swirled in his mind, jumping from awe to anger and back. He shook his head, focusing on the map in front of us.

I glanced down at the map, studying the small, almost overlapping cluster in Portland, and tapped. "This is where we need to be," I said and raised my gaze. "And by we, I mean Damian and me. Not you, just in case."

Captain O'Keefe's lips thinned as he debated, and then he slowly shook his head. "I need to be there as well. I want to nail this fucker just as much as I wanted to nail the Windwalker."

I raised an eyebrow in a silent challenge.

"Yeah, I fucked up with you, but can you blame me?" He crossed his arms, almost daring me to contradict him. "Besides, I need to sleep on this shit." He tapped his temple. "Because I really don't know how much was pure bullshit and how much was real."

"Look, I went the denial route as well, but the more we pussy-foot around, the more people will die," Steve said. "And honestly, it would be nice to have someone besides my wife to talk to about all this crap."

O'Keefe let out a laugh. "I'm never speaking of this. Not unless I want them to lock my ass up in a padded room," he said, waving towards the door and the station beyond it. "But I'm also not going to let you two screw up an investigation," he added, directing his sharp glance in my direction.

"Fine," I said aloud, although it came out just as just 'fi', but he got the gist.

"I don't know how I'm going to explain you two, though," he muttered under his breath.

"You can tell them the truth. We run a paranormal investigation firm," Damian said. "And due to the nature of the deaths, you felt a need to rule out anything... supernatural."

O'Keefe laughed. "That's as bad as enlisting a gypsy who reads tarot cards," he said when he wound down. "But with how desperate they are, maybe they'll understand."

"Is there a way to put these folks under protective custody?" I asked pointing to the three dots.

O'Keefe inhaled and shook his head. "Not without hard evidence and I certainly can't go to them with this." He held up the notebook, handing it back to me. He rubbed his face and glanced at

Steve. "I could just deputize you two," he muttered under his breath.

"We hold certain abilities that can aid in the investigation," Damian said.

"It would only hold until this case is solved," O'Keefe said.

"Works for me," I signed and transmitted.

"And it does not, I repeat, it does not authorize you to kill."

He pointed at the two of us and I nodded assent. I wasn't that hyped up to kill again. The only man I ever killed was Raven's father, and while it was ruled self-defense, however justified his death was taking a life still haunted my nightmares.

Chapter 8

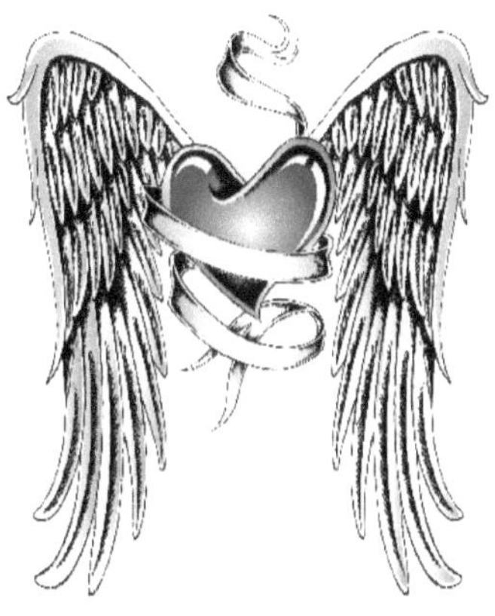

NAOMI'S CAR WAS IN the driveway, and both Damian and I sighed. I felt the smirk before I realized it even landed on my lips and we traded a glance. Our hope for a peaceful afternoon in my study, doing further research, was dashed by the reality of four toddlers running amok.

When we stepped through the door, the chaos we envisioned was real. Gabe and Michael were chasing Hannah and Grace around the house with light sabers, and the girls were shrieking in that 'I'm having so much fun' way that was ear splitting.

Raven and Naomi sat on the couch with coffee and a plate of fruit on the coffee table in front of them. I wasn't sure if the food was for them or the kids. They both looked up from their conversation when we stepped into the room.

After the last couple of hours, I really wasn't prepared for the chaos, and it set my instant irritation switch to the on position. Raven homed in on my aura before she met my gaze.

"You know what might be fun for the kids?" she asked and then turned to Naomi.

"What's that?" Naomi said, sipping her coffee.

"The playground."

At that moment, I could have given my wife a long, lingering kiss. I swear sometimes she's the one with the mind-reading abilities.

Naomi smiled and turned to Damian. "Do you mind?"

"Not at all," he said. "Do you mind if I tag along?" he asked, surprising all of us, but the sideways glance he gave me told me enough. He was not comfortable leaving his wife and kids to chance. He gave me a nod, confirming my thoughts, and his eyes wandered to Raven and Hannah, including them under his protective net.

"I think I'm just going to hang out here. Okay?" I signed and Raven crossed and planted a kiss on my cheek.

"You look like you need some rest," she whispered. "We can talk later if you'd like."

I met her gaze and gave her a smile and a nod of thanks. It took a few minutes to corral the kids and then an eerie silence settled on the house. I crossed to our bedroom and lay down on the bed. No matter what position I chose, sleep was not in the cards.

After tossing on the bed for a good hour, I decided a drink on the deck was a better idea and grabbed myself a beer from the refrigerator. I collapsed into the chase lounge and stared out at the ocean, trying to figure out all that had happened today.

While I knew there were three people on the descendant list between the latest kill and York, I couldn't help but feel uneasy, like I was sitting on a prequel to disaster. Nothing settled well, not even the beer, and I ended up trading the alcohol for a ginger ale and some fish crackers.

When Raven came home, I opted to remain outside watching the sun dance on the summer waves while she cleaned the sand off of Hannah.

When the television turned on to some PBS show and the door opened, I glanced over my shoulder at Raven.

She offered me that supportive smile, and I sighed.

"What happened at the police station?" she asked.

I didn't know where to start, so I just cut to the part I knew she would balk at. "He knows what CJ and I can do."

"Why in the name of all that is sacred…"

I held my hand up to stop the rant. "He came to me for help with a case that, on the surface, looked like something supernatural, but it's another serial killer that is making the deaths look like a fictional vampire. Of course, O'Keefe had no idea what an actual vampire looked like. At least not until I shared what happened at Paradise Cove the night the triplets were born." I signed and transmitted at the same time, staring out at the ocean instead of looking at her.

"Why would you show him that?" she gasped.

"Because Steve ordered me to. The killer we are dealing with may be in league with Lucifer."

Silence filled the space between us, and I finally glanced in her direction. Her lips were pressed tight in the familiar posture of anger, but her eyes held fear and I reached over, taking her hand in mine.

"It's not here in York," I transmitted, watching the tightness around her lips and eyes relax a fraction.

"Then why is the captain asking for your help?"

"Steve sent him to us. The Portland police asked for his help, considering he got the credit for busting the Windwalker."

Raven rolled her eyes. "Steve caught my father, not the York Police."

I nodded. If Steve hadn't done that two places in one shit, Jennifer and I would have died, and who knows what that prick would have done to Raven. "But the world doesn't know that," I signed.

"Do you trust O'Keefe to keep his mouth shut?"

I let out a laugh. "He said, and I quote, if I ever say any of this out loud, I'll end up in the loony bin." I signed and transmitted. That brought a much-needed smile to Raven's face.

"Aye, I sometimes wonder if that's where we all should be."

Her lovely smile caught on and I returned it before hers faded away.

"You aren't thinking of going after Lucifer, are you?" she asked.

I turned away from her and stared out at the ocean. My brother was a trinity, I wasn't. He was nearly killed by Lucifer before he was infused with angel grace. If he couldn't kick Lucifer's ass, I certainly couldn't. I didn't respond at first.

"Tom?"

I turned towards her. "As long as he leaves us alone, I won't go on any sort of hunting trip."

She blinked in response to the words I transmitted in her head. "You need to leave that to CJ." She crossed her arms and leaned back in the seat.

Her moody stare drilled through me, and I looked away. I wasn't about to promise her I wouldn't go after the bastard if he made good on his horrific promises. I had been through enough in my life to know that would push me over the edge for good.

"Can we not talk about this right now?" I finally asked.

The sharpness in Raven's glare softened as she studied me.

"Reliving that again rattled you, didn't it?"

I huffed and looked away. "I would expect more nightmares," I signed without looking her way. Her shift pulled my gaze back to her. Raven stood and swung a leg over my chair, taking a seat on my lap. Her arms wrapped around my neck, pulling me to her. I accepted the hug, ensnaring her just as tightly as she held me. Having her in my arms erased the horrors I'd had to recall this morning, and I couldn't help but be thankful for just how well she read my needs.

I pressed my lips to the soft nape of her neck and whispered, "I love you," in my broken tongue.

"I love you, too," she whispered back.

Instead of letting her go, I took her earlobe between my teeth and nibbled. She immediately squirmed in my arms, letting out a surprised squeal. A soft chuckle escaped from between my lips, but I didn't stop right away. I nuzzled her more, nibbling and sucking to my heart's content while her laughter rang out over the ocean.

I finally let go of her when Hannah banged on the glass door, yelling for Daddy to stop.

We both looked at our daughter with the same wide grin plastered on our faces. The worry carved in her young features transformed, and she smiled back at us before turning back to the television.

"I should spank you," Raven whispered in admonishment.

I raised an eyebrow. "Please do," I signed.

Her eyes narrowed, and she pointed at me. "Be good."

"Aren't I always?"

Blush heightened in her cheeks, and she pressed her lips against a smile. "Bad," she said and shook her head, getting off my lap.

I grinned up at her. "See what happens to me when I have a wild night with you? I just want more."

Before she turned away to head inside, I caught the smile and the silent promise to perhaps sneak another wild night in, depending on how well Hannah went down. I thought about using my unique talents to put her to sleep, but Raven would have my ass if I did that.

I closed my eyes, trying to enjoy the afternoon sun, but the moment my lids closed, my father's severed head and bloodstained wings painted the back of my eyelids. And just like that, all the heat of the day vanished, and my eyes jumped open.

I wondered what sort of manifestation the nightmares would take this time. Would it be my head tossed onto the pristine snow, or a far worse scenario?

I shivered and climbed out of the chair, heading inside to help my wife with dinner.

"What can I do?" I signed when she turned from the stove.

She pointed towards the cutting board, and the array of vegetables waiting to be chopped into a salad, without questioning why I was in the kitchen on her night. We usually trade off cooking duties while the other person is working with Hannah on reading or something equally stimulating, but Hannah was glued to the television program and I had no inclination to tear her from that to do some A-B-C's with her, or continue getting her acclimated to sign language.

I concentrated on chopping the array in front of me: Lettuce, tomatoes, cucumbers, peppers, carrots and mushrooms, throwing all the ingredients into a salad bowl and tossing before I cleaned up the cutting board and counter.

"Thank you," Raven said as she brought the pot of spaghetti to the table. "Hannah, dinner!"

Hannah came running in and neatly slid into the kitchen chair like a seasoned stuntman. She wiped the hair out of her face and then grinned at the two of us. The light in her eyes danced as she waited for us to serve her.

"What was your favorite thing that you did today?" I asked while Raven piled spaghetti with sauce on our plates and filled our salad bowls.

Hannah looked up at the ceiling; tapping her fork on her lips gently while her mind went through all the things she'd had fun doing. I was privy to the entire thought process, but I always waited until she articulated her favorite moment.

"Seeing you and mommy playing on the porch," she said, completely surprising me.

I glanced at Raven and her eyes were as wide as I imagined mine were.

"You didn't have fun with Grace, Gabe and Michael?" Raven asked.

"Yes, but Daddy asked what my favorite moment was, and it was hearing you two laugh."

I stared at my little girl, wondering when the last time I truly laughed in her presence was. I couldn't recall and Raven and I traded a glance.

When the hell had I gotten so serious?

She gave me a shoulder shrug wondering the same things I was, and at that moment, I made myself a promise. I would try harder to show my daughter that life is to be enjoyed, not overshadowed by darkness.

Chapter 9

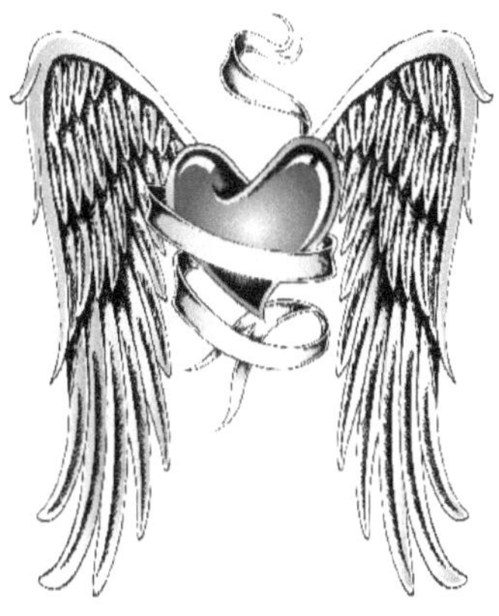

"PLEASE DON'T," RAVEN BEGGED as I approached her. She guarded Hannah, backing up with every step I took. Fear painted her features along with splattered blood.

The walls surrounding us were streaked with gore and the axe I carried dripped blood. I could feel the maniac inside advancing, but I had no control over my body and my mind screamed and pleaded for this madness to end. That I'd do anything they wanted if they would just spare my wife and child.

The floor was speckled with body parts. Arms, legs, torsos and heads of the ones I already slaughtered and all their vacant eyes were glued to my form. Devastation squeezed my insides as my gaze traveled over the familiar faces. CJ, Valerie, Alex, Steve, Jennifer and even Damian, Naomi and their children lay slain at my feet. All that was left was my wife and my child.

A maniacal laugh filled the small room as the axe came down again, slicing through Raven's delicate skin. Her blood was hot as it splashed me and the creature controlling my actions reveled in it.

Hannah's wail echoed off the walls, and I swung again, silencing the last scream.

I stood alone in a river of my family's blood and the vacant eyes of everyone I ever loved stared back.

A raspy scream shattered the silence, and I sat up in bed only to realize it was my scream. The nightmare still captured my mind, creating a terror so great I had a hard time drawing a breath.

The light brush of a hand ran across my back, and I jumped, turning towards the figure next to me. I almost struck the shape, but pulled my fist back before I smashed the face close to my shoulder.

"It's okay, it's only a nightmare," Raven said, her groggy voice cut through the fog, and I willed the lights on.

Blinking against the sudden brightness, I stared at her, horrified at the depravity of the nightmare. I shook for a good five minutes as she rubbed my back. I couldn't articulate more than a labored breath, and when my heart rate landed back in the realm of normal, I turned and wrapped my arms around her, pulling her to me so I could make sure she was really all right.

"You're crushing me," she mumbled against my chest, and I loosened my grip.

"Sorry," I whispered but still kept her in my arms to avoid the questions I knew were coming. They were already swarming in her head, and I had no words to tell my wife I dreamed of murdering her and my daughter. There was nothing remotely endearing about ending a night of passionate lovemaking with a bloodthirsty nightmare.

She squirmed, pushing back enough so she could look at my face. "Talk to me," she said, like it should be easy to share what had me so completely rattled that I didn't have the will to speak of it.

I slowly shook my head.

"Your parent's heads again?"

A near hysterical laugh escaped, and I looked at the ceiling, avoiding her gaze as I shook my head. If only it was that nightmare. As horrible as that one was, it paled compared to this violent monstrosity. This new manifestation was worse than all of my nightmares rolled into one horror fest, including the ones where Hannah was the one being carved up in Georgia.

As I stared at the swirl pattern on the drywall above me, I wondered what the hell the psychology of this dream was. They say nightmares manifest your deepest fears and this truly was the king of all nightmares.

When I brought my gaze back to hers, I drew in a deep breath, letting her out of my arms so I could sign.

"Everyone died," I started, and balled my hands into fists, clamping my eyes shut for a second. The whistle of the axe in my head made them spring back open, and I met Raven's gaze. "I killed everyone," I signed after a few minutes. "Including you and Hannah. I couldn't stop... killing."

The admission swelled in my chest, hurting the muscles in my back with the force of the breath I took. It was bad enough that I had the dream to begin with, but sharing the level of darkness that encompassed it was worse.

"I couldn't... control it."

Her palm cupped my cheek. "Do you know why you had the dream?"

I shrugged one shoulder.

"Was it the case you are working on with the police?"

"No." I was able to articulate the word, and I stared into her eyes, trying to analyze what could have triggered this. I expected a nightmare with severed heads; I just didn't expect to be the one responsible for the slaughtering.

I blinked and slipped out of bed, crossing to the sliding glass doors and staring out at the star filled sky. Was that the rationale? I felt responsible for the trail of deaths in some way?

She came up behind me and wrapped her arms around my waist, pressing gentle kisses on my slick back.

"You would never do anything like that," she said, staring over my shoulder at my reflection. I met her gaze.

I might not, but Lucifer would do it in a second, especially if he had what he wanted.

What I denied him.

Access to a body infused with the kind of magic mine had. If he had that, he could easily take out Damian. He could easily control Naomi to do his bidding and create an army of dark trinities to enslave the world. And if he ever got hold of Grace, who knows what the hell he could create.

Maybe it was all his heinous promises when I told him to go pound sand that made me feel responsible for the darkness overshadowing my family.

Maybe it was the fact that bastard's blood ran through my veins.

Maybe I was darker than I cared to admit.

I sighed and turned in her grasp, looking down into her beautiful, upturned face.

I knew I had the capacity to kill. I killed her father with no second thoughts, and I was never sure if it really was self-defense or not. Sure, he was coming at us intending to kill, but I could have disarmed him. I could have just incapacitated him, but I chose to end him with a punch to the throat.

"I don't think I'm as good as you seem to think I am," I signed.

"Bullshit, Tom. You have the heart of an angel." She swatted my chest with her hand.

I laughed. "That's what I'm afraid of."

"I'm not talking about Lucifer, you ass. I can see your aura. You can't hide your innate goodness from me, and if you had darkness inside you, I would have seen it a mile away and we would not be where we are right now."

I took a long inhalation and exhaled.

"I think I killed your father on purpose," I signed, finally admitting to something that hung heavy on my heart.

"That doesn't make you evil. That makes you human," she said. Her blue eyes were convincing enough, even without the conviction in her tone.

My lips twitched into a smile. This is why I loved this woman with every fiber of my being. She made me stronger than I really was. I pulled her into a hug.

"Come on, let's go back to bed," she said and peeled out of my arms, taking my hand in hers.

I let her lead me back to the bed, and I wrapped my arms around her, molding my body to hers. She fell asleep long before I did. While I appreciated her faith in me, I never told her I didn't immediately turn Lucifer down. I actually considered the offer, especially since it came with a promise to keep my wife and daughter safe.

It wasn't until I realized Raven would never forgive me if I sold the rest of my family out that I said no. That reason was more powerful than the possibility of having to kill my own brother and I felt like a shit heel for even considering the idea.

You see, Raven would rather die a thousand deaths than make a deal with the devil. I, on the other hand, would sell my soul to keep my family safe.

Chapter 10

THE PHONE RANG AT a little after eight and I grabbed it off the bedside table, yawning as I said, "Hey."

"Tom?" O'Keefe's voice sounded on the other end of the line.

"Ya," I said into the receiver.

"I need you and Mr. Andreas at the station in ten minutes. I think we might have another situation," He cleared his throat. "I would like you to come for a ride-along, just in case this is more than I can take on myself."

I had to force the smile onto my face as Raven rolled over and looked at me with those inquisitive eyes so full of concern. "O'a," I said, transmitting the full 'okay' so O'Keefe would know what the hell I was saying.

Ten minutes. It would take Damian that long to get halfway across York in the summer traffic. I sent him a text and then gave Raven a quick kiss before jumping out of bed for a record-breaking shower. All I smelled was sex and sweat. I didn't need to walk into the station reeking of Raven's sweet sensual perfume mixed with nightmare sweats.

The night left me feeling sluggish, seriously compromising my ability to rush. But I took the time to cross back to the bed and sit on the edge while I laced my sneakers. Flip-flops and shorts probably wouldn't have gone over well on a ride-along, so I donned a decent pair of jeans and a short-sleeved button-up shirt.

Raved kept her sleepy eyes on me and I turned my attention to her, wiping the stray wisps out of her face before I planted a kiss on her forehead and then lips.

"We're heading to Portland to investigate another missing person." I signed and caressed her cheek. "I'll be back as soon as I can."

"Just promise you'll be careful," she said.

I gave her a nod. "Love you," I signed and stood, heading out of the bedroom to her soft response.

When I pulled into the station, both Damian and O'Keefe stood outside, leaning on one of the police cruisers with their arms crossed. I gave them a half shrug as I crossed the distance.

"I said ten minutes," O'Keefe snapped.

"Sorry," I muttered and transmitted, blocking all of my rationale from Damian's probing stare.

"Just get in the damned car," he said, and stepped to the driver's side.

"I can't believe I got here before you did," Damian muttered and handed me a coffee after he slid into the front seat.

I grunted my thanks and sent the sign for sorry, again.

I spent the rest of the ride letting the caffeine do its thing and wake me up. The closer we got, the more on edge I got. It didn't stop, even when we pulled into the driveway. We got out of the cruiser at the house and every nerve in my body thrummed. My stomach dropped and I couldn't pinpoint what the issue was, but things were not right.

And then I saw the shimmering shadow, and I sighed, even before O'Keefe could knock on the door. Damian came up short as well and his gaze shot to mine like he was seeing what I was seeing. The ghost of the latest victim looked out the window at us as we approached.

"We are already too late," I transmitted, and O'Keefe looked over his shoulder at me, his finger poised over the doorbell.

His eyes followed mine, and he huffed at the empty window. He didn't see the ghost that stared at me, and his finger stabbed the doorbell.

I traded a glance with the ghost of Mrs. Freeman, trying to convey just how sorry I was.

The door opened seconds later, and a frantic Mr. Freeman stared at us. O'Keefe pulled out his badge and Mr. Freeman's gaze hardened.

"It's about time they sent someone over. I've been calling you people since last night. There is no way Ellie would have just run off."

O'Keefe glanced at us, but I was too preoccupied with the ghost that now stood in the entryway behind Mr. Freeman.

"Where?" I signed, like the ghost could relay the information, but she just stared with wide eyes and a gaping maw. The holes in her neck were bruised, almost as if a machine was used to suck out every drop of blood from her body.

"When did you last see her?" O'Keefe asked.

"She went out to pick up some milk at the store around eight, and that was the last time I saw her. When she wasn't home by nine, I knew something wasn't right. She didn't answer her cell phone either, and that is not like my wife." His eyes darted between Damian and O'Keefe before falling on me. "What's wrong with him?"

My gaze shifted from the ghost of his wife to him.

"He's a psychic that we employ for missing person cases," O'Keefe explained.

The man's eyebrows arched in response.

"Especially where finding the missing person quickly is paramount to their survival."

I ignored the blatant stare, moved my gaze back to Mrs. Freeman, and signed. "I am going to need your help to bring you home."

She just shrugged her shoulders. "I don't know where he has me."

"Can you give me anything to go on?"

She looked up at the ceiling and tapped her lips. "When I got back into my car, I felt a sting on my neck and I saw a shadow in the backseat, but before I could turn, I lost control of all my muscles."

I raised an eyebrow. The only time I can recall something acting that fast had to be in Steve's memory banks when the Slasher drugged him. He was aware, but couldn't control his muscles.

"I couldn't feel a thing," she added softly.

That differed from Steve's ordeal. He felt every horror that man rained on him.

"But you were awake?"

"Yes."

"Did you see who or what was responsible?"

She shook her head.

"He blindfolded me and moved me into the passenger seat. I couldn't speak and I couldn't move, but I could hear." She swallowed. "I could hear his plans for me," she added, in only a whisper.

I waited as her image shimmered in and out; her hold waning, repelled by fear. Fear made ghosts disappear, and I didn't push because I needed her to remain tangible, to remain talking.

After a few moments, she solidified again, and I asked, "Was it a big space or small space?"

She cocked her head, thinking. "There was an echo, so I think it might have been big, and it smelled like mold."

"A basement?" I signed, transmitting to the ghost.

She shrugged. "Now all I smell is seaweed."

I exhaled and closed my eyes, hanging my head. If she smelled the ocean, that meant the killer had already dumped the body and was targeting the next victim. I opened my eyes and moved my glance to Damian. He held the same stoic expression, except I recognized the building alarm in his eyes.

"We will do everything we can to bring your wife home to you, but I'm afraid we may already be too late," I signed, and Damian translated for me.

Mr. Freeman's expression slowly fell, and tears filled his eyes. I purposely did not listen to his morbid thoughts; instead, I gave him a nod and turned, heading back to the car. I slid into the passenger seat and waited for Damian and O'Keefe to return to the car.

Chapter 11

"WHAT THE HELL WAS that all about?" O'Keefe asked, after he closed the driver's door, sending a glare my way.

"She's already dead," I signed, without the additional transmission. "We need to go to where the others were found." I added, and Damian was kind enough to translate.

O'Keefe glanced at me. "Are you sure?"

"He was talking to her ghost," Damian said.

O'Keefe glanced at Damian in the rearview mirror before sending his sharp stare in my direction. "Did you ask if she could identify the killer?" His tone was as condescending as I remembered when I was seventeen.

I glared at him and crossed my arms. "I'm a damned good investigator, Captain." The thought barreled out, and he winced.

"Did you ask?" he said through clenched teeth.

"You really think I'm an idiot, don't you?" It was my turn to snap, and I transmitted at full volume just out of aggravation. The physical discomfort written on his scrunched features made me soften my tone. I needed him functional and not blinded by a migraine from my recklessness. "Of course, I asked. And no, she didn't see her attacker, but she said she felt something like a bite on her neck and within seconds, she couldn't move. She was blindfolded and brought to a damp and dark area that echoed. I'm guessing a large basement or even an abandoned mill of some sort."

O'Keefe started the car and headed towards Wright's Warf. There was already a circus of police lights when we pulled in. The three of us got out.

"Stay here until I find out what is going on," O'Keefe ordered, and Damian and I exchanged a glance, but we stayed put.

O'Keefe stepped into the chaos, leaving Damian and me standing next to the car like a pair of junior detectives not cleared for a homicide case. I closed my eyes, choosing to infringe upon the conversation he was having with the lead officer.

Get out of my head. O'Keefe's thought overshadowed the conversation, and I opened my eyes, catching his glare. I sent a smirk in response, but it quickly faded with the next set of facts.

Two people were found in the same condition, both bled dry and tossed out like a sack of garbage.

My gaze snapped to Damian, but he had already pulled his phone from his pocket and was busy dialing home. His warning was simple. Get to my brother's house with the family.

I followed suit, texting Raven to do the same and then followed with a warning to CJ. His response came before my wife's and I felt a moment of relief until Raven's text popped up.

I'll head over as soon as Hannah wakes from her nap.

My gut clenched. Our house was the farthest north and the first this psycho would hit if he continued his systematic elimination of angel blood. I didn't want to alarm her, but I also didn't want her vulnerable and every nerve in my body shouted to get her out of the house.

There was only one person left between Portland and York, and she was in Ogunquit. Just a fifteen-minute ride from our place. I took a seat in the car and gave Damian a quick glance before I bowed my head and did the one thing I vowed I'd never do again. I projected myself into my house.

Raven glanced up at my image and her eyebrows formed that surprised arc that always made me smile, but it fell short this time. I didn't have time to enjoy her cuteness and my lack of a smile formed a frown on her face.

"I need you to wake her and go now," I signed.

Her features transformed, and she crossed her arms. "I most certainly will not," she said in that stubborn Irish brogue.

I inhaled, trying to calm the building annoyance. "Hannah is in danger," I signed slowly, watching her turn from that stubborn jut of her chin to wide-eyed panic.

Her gaze locked with mine and there were no more questions. She gave a nod, and I felt the pull back to the car an hour away from my daughter.

When I opened my eyes, O'Keefe was sitting in the driver's seat, just staring at me.

Damian was already seated in the back as the car idled.

"What?" I transmitted.

"Damian said, uh, he said you stepped out for a minute."

I nodded and pointed for us to get moving.

"The names match the list," Damian said quietly as O'Keefe pulled back on the road.

I already knew that. I also had a sneaking suspicion that all this was staged in some way, and I glanced in the mirror at Damian. He sent me an imperceptible nod, telling me we were both on the same page.

"Is that what your brother looked like at the other end?" O'Keefe asked.

"Ya," I said.

"It never ceases to freak me the fuck out," Damian said from the back seat, pulling a chuckle from O'Keefe.

"Imagine actually doing it," I transmitted, keeping my eyes on the passing scenery.

"I can't," O'Keefe mumbled under his breath.

Neither one of them could grasp the feeling. CJ and I share the same distaste for astral projection. I'm not sure my mother ever got used to it either, but both my father and Steve used it as a weapon. To them, it offered a profound sense of security, but to me, it just magnified what kind of an inhuman freak I had become.

Chapter 12

O'KEEFE'S PHONE RANG JUST as we crossed through the tolls back into York. He listened, sighed, and hung up. Without enlightening us to the content of the call, he swung off the southbound side of the highway and immediately re-entered on the northbound side, heading back the way we came, except instead of the long drive back to Portland, he took the first exit for Wells, turning south on Route 1 and backtracking to the Ogunquit town line.

My heart rammed against my ribcage as we pulled to a stop over the Ogunquit River. The latest body was dumped over the side of Route 1 into the river. When I saw the arm hanging out of the body bag, my throat closed. This body had been there for a while, certainly longer than the bodies dumped in Portland this morning, and that scared the hell out of me.

"We have to get home," I signed to Damian. It had only been a couple of hours since we'd left Portland, but with every second that passed, the alarms inside my head clamored louder.

He exhaled and glanced at O'Keefe talking with the Ogunquit police.

I shot off a text to Raven, telling her where I was and that I'd be a little longer, and then refocused on O'Keefe. When the name of the victim surfaced, I glanced at Damian. His reaction confirmed it. He wiped his face and leaned against the car, defeat written into the lines surrounding his eyes.

Whoever this killer was, he was operating with a playbook that was several steps ahead of us. I glanced at my phone, expecting the usual 'k' from Raven, but nothing had been returned. The unease increased to a silent tension that wrapped around my midsection like a python squeezing the life out of me.

I sent a text off to CJ asking if Raven had gotten there. His response took me out at the knees and I grabbed for the hood of the car to steady myself. My mind clouded over at the morbid possibility and my feet moved of their own accord. Before I was even aware of what I was doing, I was in the driver's seat, turning the ignition key.

Damian slid into the front passenger seat. "You can't steal O'Keefe's car," he said. "Give him a second."

I stared at him like he had lost his mind, and then the driver's door opened.

"Get in back," O'Keefe said.

I clenched my teeth, but something told me I shouldn't be the one driving right now and I relinquished the seat. Before I closed the back door, O'Keefe hit the gas. He went full board with lights and sirens, and the way he drove earned him an ounce of respect.

"The last time you saw her was when we were in Portland, correct?" he asked without taking his eyes from the road.

"Yes," I transmitted. "She agreed to go to my brother's house, but she hasn't gotten there yet," I added. "And she didn't answer my text."

O'Keefe's eyes moved to mine in the rearview mirror. "You have the ability to check the house. Do it."

I blinked, feeling foolish for not thinking of it myself, but I nodded and closed my eyes, concentrating on home. The pull started in the center of my chest, and I opened my eyes to my empty living room. All the rooms were empty, and her day-trip bag was gone as well. She always took that whenever she was going to be anywhere for a period. I crossed and opened the front door. The car was gone.

I closed it and crossed to the garage entrance just to make sure and the garage was equally empty as everything else. My heart pounded in my throat and my breathing started that short rasp of panic. The pull yanked me back to the car and my wild eyes met O'Keefe's in the rearview mirror.

"She's not there. Neither is her car."

"Color, make, model, and license plate," O'Keefe barked at me.

"Blue Ford Explorer, RAVEN."

O'Keefe nodded and picked up his radio microphone. "I have a report of a stolen vehicle. Blue Ford Explorer, Maine, Romeo, Alpha, Victor, Echo, November. I need this to go out on an APB right now."

The dispatcher on the other end repeated the information back and assured O'Keefe that the bulletin would go out immediately. He replaced the microphone in the holder and glanced at me.

"Thank you," I said with my mind and the proper sign language gesture.

He gave a curt nod and focused. Twenty minutes later, we pulled into my still empty driveway, and I headed inside, hoping things had changed since I projected into the house less than a half hour before.

"Is she there yet?" I texted to CJ.

The phone rang, and I snatched it off the wall.

"No, but everyone else is. What do you need from me?" CJ asked.

I scanned the house with my heart pounding in my throat, unsure of how to answer him. I needed my wife and daughter and an icy fear spilled into my body, freezing me in place.

"Tom, it will be okay," he said softly, but he stopped short of adding a promise. "Steve's already out looking for her."

I traded a glance with Damian and O'Keefe standing in the entryway.

"Thanks," I transmitted and hung up and closed my eyes wondering why my wife wouldn't call me if she was in danger.

The harsh truth bit at every centimeter of my skin. She was dead, or the madman threatened Hannah. Raven would do anything for our daughter, even if it put herself in harm's way.

Chapter 13

I GLANCED AT THE house as we pulled into the driveway. CJ stood in the open doorway, looking more tired than I've ever seen him. He knew something of the panic assaulting me, so did Damian. I had already decided. As soon as Damian was with his family, I was going hunting for this bastard.

I didn't plan on going inside, and from the way O'Keefe lingered by the car, I got the same sense of urgency from him. He had had enough exposure to my wife in the aftermath of the Windwalker case to have a small soft spot for her, and he was damned if he'd let this killer terrorize his town.

"Take a fly by later," I sent to Damian as he stepped next to my brother. He sent a nod. Once it was dark, he'd transform into a giant hawk and take a once over. From an aerial vantage point, he might see something those of us on the ground would miss.

The radio squawked in the car as I slid into the passenger seat, but O'Keefe didn't bother answering right away. Instead, he glanced at me. "You sure you don't want to stay with your family?"

"I can't just sit still," I transmitted. "And you know damned well that if I'm not with you, I'd end up hunting on my own. Then you'd probably throw my ass in jail."

He sent a half smile in my direction with a nod. "You're probably right," he said, and picked up the radio microphone. "O'Keefe here."

"We found the car in Hannaford's parking lot, sir," the dispatcher said.

"I'm on my way," he replied and spun the car around, heading out without any further delay.

When we got to Hannaford's, the police had sectioned off the farthest corner and our SUV sat in the second to last space. The forensics team was already combing through the vehicle for evidence.

Steve stood by the crew, scanning computer results; he looked over the roof of the car, directly at me, as I got out of the car. The concern in his eyes made me pause. He gave a nod to the officer and stepped around to meet me before I got close.

"You shouldn't be here," he said and sent a glare towards O'Keefe.

I pulled out the deputy shield O'Keefe had given me and raised an eyebrow.

"You are too close to the case," Steve said in response.

"Tell us what you found," O'Keefe said to the approaching detective.

The detective raised an evidence bag containing a needle. "This contains traces of etorphine," he said in a tone that I didn't understand. O'Keefe sucked air through his teeth, and I glanced at him.

"What the hell is etorphine?" I signed and transmitted, and Steve grabbed my arm, leading me away as O'Keefe conferred with the rest of the forensic team.

"It's used by veterinarians to knock out big animals."

I stared at him, waiting for the rest.

"It knocks out humans like that," he snapped his fingers. "And can be fatal if the antidote isn't given within a matter of hours." He shoved his hands in his pocket and dropped his gaze to the ground. "We think he must have had a van because no one in the parking lot noticed him transferring Raven or Hannah from the car."

Before I could ask anything else, a sound echoed, like someone had set off a firework display. Over the trees toward York Harbor, a black plume of smoke rolled into the sky. All activity in the parking lot stopped for a second, and then the chatter started on all the radios. O'Keefe moved away, pointing for the team to continue what they were doing, and he waved for both Steve and me. The address of the explosion rang through the scanners and before I knew it, both Steve and I were in a dead run.

The address was my brother's house. Where most of the angel blood congregated. Shit.

Steve didn't bother with O'Keefe's car; he was in his little BMW flying out of the parking lot before we even backed out of our spot. A second explosion rocked the road as we turned the corner onto

Roaring Rock. I stared at the two towers of smoke so closely aligned and let out my breath.

As we turned the bend, approaching the iron gates that once held my family's home, smoldering rubble met my gaze. The house next door was in the same condition and the fire trucks had beaten us to the location.

Steve's car was stopped in the middle of the road and empty. The door hung open as he stood on the lawn with his hands threaded through his hair.

"We're in back," CJ's thought crept into my mind, and I exhaled, leaning back in the passenger seat while a wave of relief swept through me. O'Keefe pulled to a stop, and I got out, crossing to Steve and signing their location. He didn't wait for me; instead, he bolted around the cleared side of the house. I followed, with O'Keefe on my heels.

As we passed onto the back lawn, CJ had Alex in his arms and Valerie stood by his side. Both of them just stared at what remained of their house. Damian and his family stood close by and Jennifer sat on the rock wall, just as stunned as the rest of them.

The debris field was more to the front than the backyard and I stared at the untouched pool and the expanse of green lawn before turning and looking at the rubble of the home I grew up in.

"What happened?" Steve asked, as he skidded to a stop in front of Jennifer.

She just shrugged.

"I had less than a minute to get everyone out of the house, between Jennifer's vision and the explosion," CJ said, still staring at the house.

I started toward CJ and when I was halfway across the lawn, a third explosion in the distance pulled all our gazes to the left. Across town, on the bluff, another plume of smoke colored the sky. My stomach dropped as I watched smoke billow from the exact location of our home.

All our memories reduced to rubble, and my gaze bounced back to CJ's. The war had started in earnest, and we knew who was directing the troops against us. Just the thought of Lucifer calling the shots burned through my shock and I clenched my fists.

The promises he'd made to both CJ and me regarding my family shook me to the core, and the urgency to find my wife overrode all the destruction around me. They had to be in town still.

I just had to figure out where.

Chapter 14

O'KEEFE ASSEMBLED US IN one of the larger meeting rooms at the station, leaving us to our own devices while he sent his deputies out to get us something to eat and drink.

"What are you doing about all this?" I signed, as O'Keefe entered the room with a stack of pizza boxes. He was followed in by another officer with a tray of drinks. He placed the boxes on the table.

"We're taking a closer look at the veterinarians in the area that have access to etorphine."

"And how many have access?" Steve asked as he opened the nearest box and dug into the pizza.

O'Keefe looked away and cleared his throat. "There are only two on record between here and Portland. York Wild Kingdom and the first victim up in Portland." He returned his gaze to mine. "They think some of the drug is missing from the victim's office."

Shit. I pressed my lips together, trying to clear my mind of all thoughts. I stood and crossed to the window, glancing out at the dwindling light. It had been six hours since I saw Raven in our house. A body could be drained of blood in six hours, and yet if she was dead, I was certain her ghost would have found me by now.

There were precious few large remote areas around here and even fewer abandoned ones. With the way this guy was killing, the outdoors wasn't the place to do this, especially during the summer when the risk of hikers and trail riders was high. Which led me back to abandoned buildings.

"Eat something," Steve said as he stepped next to me, handing me a plate with a couple of slices of pizza.

The last thing I wanted to do was feed the acid burn in my stomach, but I took the plate, anyway. I kept silent and took a few bites before Steve put his hand on my shoulder. His silent support didn't help.

"I need to find them," I projected.

He nodded, but before he could speak, Jennifer gasped behind us. We spun, and I had just a moment to view her eyes—the milky eyes of precognition—before her vision assaulted me.

"WHAT HAVE YOU DONE with my daughter?" Raven's soft Irish lilt fell in the low light as the bonds holding her in place tightened. She shifted and tried to twist her wrists against the bindings, but she had no wiggle room. Her knees were bound to handles on the table at her sides. Her ankles were tethered as well and her range of motion for her lower legs was perhaps a couple of inches. The way this madman bound her left her exposed.

The chill caressing her bare skin gave her an indication of either air conditioning or being in a basement. The space wasn't huge, but it was bigger than the average cellar. A hint of ammonia filled the air, along with an underlying smell of feces, even though what she could see was clean.

"Don't worry your pretty head about that right now, sweetheart," he said, pushing her hair away from her face with a gloved hand. The lamp on his hardhat only gave her a sense of a figure, and he wasn't a small man by any means.

She caught a hint of a tattoo on his forearm before he pulled his hand away. But she couldn't identify it; just a blur of color, and then it was gone.

"Let her go," Raven begged. "You can do anything you want to me, but please don't hurt my little girl."

"Sorry, princess, she's on the list," the killer said, his voice flat with no discernible accent.

"What list?" Raven asked, trying to keep him talking. If he was talking, maybe that would buy Hannah some time.

"The same one that dictates exactly what has to be done with you."

"And what is that?"

The rolling of an industrial sized barrel crossed the smooth floor into her line of sight. He righted it, peeled the cover off, shining his headlamp into the container as he reached in and took a handful. When he lifted it into view and let the sharp red and black stones filter through his fingers, she knew exactly what the barrel held.

"Blood stone?" she asked, as confusion clouded her mind.

The light flashed in her direction, blinding her. "Yes, ma'am," he replied, and reached down, picking up a package from the floor, and put it on a small table near her. When the box opened, he huffed a laugh. "My boss has a really twisted sense of humor," he said and pulled one item out to show her. The smooth shaft caught the light and Raven gasped.

"That's apparently the last item I get to use," he said with a chuckle, shifting the paper next to the box before returning the obscene dildo to the table. The next item he picked up looked like an industrial-powered calking gun. He unthreaded the cap from the tube, twisting it off and scooped some rocks from the barrel in his hand, dropping them into the cap. She watched as they easily fell through the hole.

"That'll do." He crossed to the table and put the cap next to her head. A ripping sound followed, and duct tape covered her mouth.

"I can't have you screaming to wake the dead while I stuff you with rocks, now can I?"

"JENNIFER," STEVE'S VOICE CUT through the vision.

The plate fell from my hand, and I bolted. I had no idea where I was going, but I needed air. I needed not to hurl what little I ate, and I didn't stop running until I was standing knee deep in the water at Short Sands.

My breath hitched harshly in my chest as the horror of what was happening to my wife settled into every fiber of my body. Lucifer had threatened to stuff her with bloodstone until her intestines burst and that was exactly the intent in Jennifer's vision.

The cold water bit at my legs, reminding me of where I was. I turned to head back to the police station and take this investigation to the next level. I couldn't let that vision happen.

CJ stood in the water behind me, his face as ashen as mine must have been.

"Jesus. I am so sorry," he started, and I shoved him with everything I had.

He went down with a splash.

"She isn't dead, yet!" I screamed in my inarticulate tongue. My face heated with the building fury. "Don't fucking talk like she is dead!"

CJ climbed to his feet and put his hands out. "Calm down."

"Calm down?" I snapped with a glare.

He let out a nervous laugh. "Not the best choice of words, but I need your head clear. I'm too fucking exhausted to see straight, never mind analyze what was in that vision. I need you to put aside your panic and everything else assaulting you and get your fucking head clear."

"Why?" I couldn't help but growl.

"You need to look at what we just saw with as much objectivity as you can muster," he said, pointing at me. "Because there has to be some kind of clue as to where she is. We need to figure that out before he gets that god awful machine going."

I blinked at him, trying to shed my wife's palpable fear. She had no idea what he meant by Hannah being on the list, but I did, and it chilled me to the core. My horror was nearly as debilitating as hers, and I didn't even know if my daughter was still alive.

"We need to walk through everything, Tom," CJ said as he wrung the hem of his shirt out.

I stared at him for a few minutes before I started walking up the shore. "I don't know if I can." Tears blurred the Goldenrod sign, and I hung my head. "She was terrified."

His hand landed on my neck, and he pulled me into a hug. "I know, but she needs us to figure out the clues she fed to us. You know damned well she's operating under the assumption that we're going to see what's happening at some point. She knew Jennifer and Steve were in town."

I stepped out of his awkward embrace and stared at him. Getting hold of the beast raging inside me was easier in theory than reality, but he was right. I had to put my shit-show aside and focus.

I took a seat in the sand, shuffling it through my fingers as I went through the vision in slow motion. CJ sat next to me, filtering through what Jennifer fed us in the same way, keeping his mind open to me as to his observations. I did the same.

"Did you see... fencing?" I asked as I scanned the room through Raven's eyes.

"Chain link?"

"Yeah, on the perimeter of one side."

CJ glanced at me biting his lower lip with a nod.

"What the fuck?" I asked and then shook my head to clear it again. The clock was not our friend, and the longer it took us to pinpoint her surroundings, the longer it would take to get her out of there, before catastrophic damage was done.

"Does it seem familiar to you?" CJ asked.

I shook my head, but something at the back of my mind tickled. I did another slow scan of the memory and then sat up straight up, like the lights suddenly flipped on.

"It's a kennel." I signed and snapped my head in CJ's direction. His eyes widened.

"But it's not a normal one. The kennels on the inside are limited, almost like a temporary shelter," he added. His gaze dropped to the sand, and the crease between his eyes deepened.

"Either way, we need to let O'Keefe know," I said, getting to my feet. I offered my hand to CJ and helped him up.

We jogged back to the station and entered through the same door I'd left. The family looked up at us as I glanced around for O'Keefe, but he wasn't in the room.

"I told him I thought the killer had her in a kennel or some kind of animal shelter, and they are out looking right now," Jennifer said. Her eyes were bloodshot, like she had been crying.

Valerie crossed and deposited Alex in CJ's arms before she turned to me. "When you go, you have to take me. I can fix whatever damage they've done."

I stared into my sister-in-law's sincere eyes and slowly nodded. As much as I didn't want to put her in harm's way, she had the God-given gift of healing. And my wife and daughter may need that miracle edge to survive.

"Val," CJ interrupted, but her warning glare shut him down.

"She's my best friend," she said. That's all she needed to say.

The bond between Raven and Valerie was stronger than blood, and had been since Valerie walked into our house. They'd clicked in a way that Naomi and Valerie never had, and now she shared my panic. I felt it radiating off her, and I'm sure she felt mine just as acutely.

Chapter 15

"HOW LONG AGO DID they leave?" I signed, meeting Steve's gaze. I had been pacing enough so that the wet fabric of my jeans had started to chafe. I thought about getting a change of clothes and then remembered that I had nothing left to change into. At least not in York and a slow burning anger surfaced.

Steve glanced at his watch and stood, disappearing into the heart of the station, leaving us without much of an answer. Time wasn't something I was accustomed to measuring and right now, a second felt like an eternity. I had no idea what qualified as a minute or an hour. Either way, the longer I paced, the more unsettled I became.

I finally ripped open the door to the station and scanned the group; zeroing in on Steve at the far side of the room. I crossed and took the space next to him, looking down at the map spread on the desk.

"I got it. It looks like you've covered all the kennels in the area," he said into the phone. "Did you check the zoo?" He nodded and sighed, rubbing his face for a minute. "Thanks for the update," he added and hung up the phone before he corralled me back into the room.

"They've been to every kennel and vet office in town, including the zoo. Nothing," he said, looking between Jennifer and I. "Are you sure it was a kennel?"

I exchanged a glance with her and CJ and then closed my eyes, willing my brain to search the scene for more clues. My eyes snapped open.

"Maybe the fencing we saw was more for a storage area?" I signed but CJ was shaking his head.

"It was familiar to both of us, Tom," he said, staring at me like he was missing something, too. "Where else did we take Sam?" he asked and just the reference to my father's dog opened the floodgates of memories.

I turned to Steve. "I doubt it would be Petsmart."

He huffed a small laugh.

The one place Sam became completely disobedient was that store. I remember being pulled down aisle after aisle until Sam found what he wanted. The memory brought a smile to my lips, but the reality of our situation made it fleeting.

"The only other place we brought him was the groomers," I said, looking up.

CJ and I locked eyes, and ours both widened, before we could say anything, Steve spun on his heel and marched back to the desk he was at before. The officer overseeing the coordination effort looked up at him as he relayed the information. There were three groomers that we took Sam to over the years we had him, and I tried to remember where they were in town.

"They'll look into it," Steve said when he stepped back in the room.

"I can't just sit around and wait," I signed.

"You can, and you will," Steve said, pointing at me.

The last time I intervened in a case, I ended up in jail as a suspect.

"Fine, but if we hear nothing in the next half hour, I'm going to start looking myself."

"You can't go off half-cocked," Steve said, staring me down.

He didn't need to remind me of the last time I took matters into my own hands. I was already painfully aware of that mistake.

"The hell I can't." I returned his hard glare.

"With what?" Steve asked.

I pressed my lips together and pulled my car keys out of my pocket. "I drove here this morning." I signed and shoved them back in my pocket.

"Then I'm going with you," he said.

At least if I was with him, my affinity for getting into trouble might be tempered. The same thought paraded through his mind, and I nodded. "Okay," I signed, and this time I actually glanced at a clock in order to get a beat on the passage of time.

I slowly paced the room, trying not to disturb the baby sleeping on Valerie's chest on the couch in the corner. Her eyes drooped as well, and I traded a glance with CJ, cocking my head in their direction. He nodded in response. The collective communication between the two of us could be summed up by head shakes and shoulder shrugs, but we both knew what was going on in each other's heads.

The fact neither he nor Steve promised things would be okay was an indication of how grave this was. I couldn't face the possibility that I might lose my wife and child today. Every time that thought surfaced, panic overrode my bloodstream, and I focused on something else.

Damian's kids were all quietly coloring at the table. It was as if they knew this wasn't the place to run around like the wild children they usually were. Grace looked up and gave me a strained smile. I wanted to ask her why she smiled at me like that, but Steve tapped my shoulder and then his wrist.

Time was up and we both slid out into the heart of the station, leaving the rest of them in the quiet calm that pervaded the room. We stopped at the desk.

"Any word?" Steve asked.

"Not yet," the young officer answered.

"We're stepping out for a few," Steve said and got a nod in response. As soon as we cleared the door, he looked at me and said, "I'm driving." He didn't say anything more until we were seated in the car. "Where to?"

I pulled out my phone and searched dog groomer. There was one right down the street from the police station, one right near Hanniford's, and one on Woodbridge. I showed the three to Steve.

"We can hit the closest one and then go to the one near Hanniford's." He glanced at me, and I nodded. After all, Raven's car was found at the Hanniford's lot. I almost asked him to forego the closest place, but I saw the benefit of being systematic.

We slowed down at the sight of the police car in the driveway, but the officers were talking to the owner at the door.

"They've already done a walk-through of the place," I said, catching pieces of their thoughts. "It's clear."

Steve nodded and headed out to Route 1. The second shop was dark, and the parking lot was empty. Even though this was the closest one to where Raven was last seen, it didn't have the right vibe. We pulled into the lot behind the building and got out of the car.

"They share the building with other businesses," I signed and transmitted, and glanced at Steve. He nodded.

"We should still have a look, just in case," he said, approaching the door. He turned towards me. "Can you do the honors?" he asked, pointing at the locked door.

I closed my eyes, concentrating on unlocking the door. It was an easy lock to mentally pick, and the door popped open. The moment we stepped inside, I knew this was not the place. It was far too small to house the kill room I saw in Jennifer's vision.

"This isn't it," I said, transmitting the words, but Steve still did a quick walk-through.

"That leaves the one on Woodbridge," he said as he locked the door and closed it behind him.

The stress had my muscles knotted. If the one on Woodbridge wasn't it, I was all out of ideas and I didn't think there was much time left. Too many minutes had passed since Jennifer's vision and if that marked when the bastard started his torture, he would have long finished by now and that thought scared the living daylights out of me.

Steve gave my shoulder a pat as he navigated back toward York Harbor and Woodbridge Street.

The only thought looping through my head was that we were out of time.

Chapter 16

O'KEEFE'S TRUCK SAT IN the small parking lot in front of the last dog-grooming place and we pulled into the parking lot next to his cruiser. We got out, and I put my hand on the hood. The vehicle was cold, and I shot Steve a glance.

"It's cold." We both looked at the building on high alert. The front door of the dog grooming shop hung ajar and as we approached, Steve pulled out his service revolver and put his hand out for me to cover the rear.

"I'll go first, just back me up if the shit hits the fan, okay?" Steve whispered, and clicked off his safety.

While I had the power to level the building, he had the skill and experience to clear each room without potential harm to either himself or any innocent in the building. I was so wound up that if I went first, I might toast the first person I stumbled on. I gave him a nod and reeled my nerves in as I followed him through the door.

The front waiting room and reception desk met our slow scan as our eyes adjusted to the dark. The usually brightly lit entry was eerily dressed in shadows and Steve quickly covered the space, making sure he targeted corners and under the counters. It took him seconds to clear the room, and he ended his sweep at the side of the door leading to the grooming area and the kennels beyond.

"Clear," he whispered, and both our gazes landed on the adjoining door. The small window was shrouded in darkness and didn't give us any indication of activity. Steve took a glance through the glass, but he shook his head, counting on his fingers to three before moving into the space.

The door was spring-loaded and swung closed before I could get through the space and by the time I pushed the door open again, Steve was writhing in the center of the room, hissing and spouting foul curses. With the racket he was making, I figured whatever stealth approach we were attempting was already foiled, and I willed all the lights in the place to turn on.

Bright lights momentarily blinded me, but when my vision cleared, my gaze locked on the writhing mass in the center of the room and it took a moment to figure out what was all over Steve. A trap door in the ceiling had opened and dropped a shitload of snakes on him. And they were in full attack mode, biting like there was no tomorrow. Shock turned into a burning panic because I had no idea how to pinpoint the power I held. If I tried to annihilate the snakes, I could very well take Steve right along with them.

Instead of attacking all at once, I focused on each creature, one at a time, flinging them into the wall with deadly force. I stopped counting after twenty, and while freeing him from the attacking reptiles only took five minutes, Steve dropped to his knees, unable to make it as far as any of the others.

His breath wheezed, and the gun dropped from his grip. I looked at the other bodies. Two officers lay still, and closer to the other door lay Captain O'Keefe, just as still as the others, and I gulped down the burn of bile.

Steve interrupted my blatant stare with a raspy, "Go." He heaved the word out just before he collapsed, but his eyes moved from me to the door and back.

The horror of seeing Steve incapacitated raked through me, and a sliver of guilt rammed my chest as I stepped beyond him, picking up his gun. I crossed to the door. When I glanced back in his direction, his eyes were still tracking me and his mind echoed his last order.

I nodded and closed my eyes, sending out an SOS to Valerie. We had left the station without her, but I knew she would be on high alert, just as much as I was right now. I owed Steve a fighting chance.

"Help is on the way," I transmitted to him.

"Go. Now," his voice reprimanded me, and I turned back to the door, showing the same care he had when he entered the building. "Be careful," his whisper caught me before I pushed through the door and I glanced back at him with a nod.

I would not take any chances. Not after the trap I'd just navigated. I took a second to gather my strength and imagined building a force field around me that would protect me from falling snakes or any other booby traps that may be set between me and my family.

When I was sure I had enough of a shield in place, I swung the door open and stepped through with the gun at the ready. The overhead lights showed me the situation in prime detail and I had to concentrate to keep from dropping to my knees.

Raven was tied to a metal table that looked like the one I had been strapped to in Georgia, but it was tipped at a forty-five degree angle. The duct tape remained across her mouth, keeping her whimpers almost silent. Her arms were stretched over her head and her legs were hip distance apart and tied to the edge of the table. Her abdomen looked like someone had taken a baseball bat to it and drops of blood ran in slow paths down the insides of her legs.

Pain filled her eyes, and her voice echoed in my head. "Trap."

I took a step forward, right into a wire, and the bastard had the audacity to smile before a wall of fire and debris filled my vision. The roar that followed almost drowned Raven's wail of anguish. Heat wrapped around me, but retreated just as quickly. Shrapnel hovered, impaled in my invisible shield, blocking my view, and I snarled; turning what should have ripped me to shreds into a dust cloud.

My wife's captor was no longer smiling. Instead, his jaw hung open and his dark eyes widened. He looked like every cliché mercenary I had ever seen in the movies. Built like a two-ton truck, and I hoped he was just as dumb.

I stepped farther into the room, refocusing the gun on the bastard. That seemed to unlock his paralysis, and he stepped closer to Raven, putting a blade across her throat.

I took a quick glance to my left, validating there was no other trap, and my gaze locked on my little girl. Hannah hung by her feet with her arms bound at her side. Her face was almost purple from the blood pooling in her head. A tube ran from her throat, emptying into a gallon sized milk jug. What alarmed me the most was that the container was almost half-full, and my gaze snapped back to the madman.

"Mother fucker," I said, but my inability to articulate just made it sound like an animal's feral growl. I gathered the fury into a tight ball in my chest, focusing.

Raven gave a slight shake of her head. "Save Hannah," she whispered, but I ignored her, willing the knife pressed into her throat to move away from her skin.

Despite the killer's taut muscles, the knife pulled away, and I had a moment where I believed saving them both was possible.

"My boss said you were a force to be reckoned with," he said, and before I could react, he raised his free hand, pushing the button on the remote detonator in his hand.

Movement to my left pulled my attention before I could harness the power into something that would save us all. Instead, I reacted, sending a force field around Hannah just in time to stop a pendulum blade from slicing her in half. It stilled an inch from her face and kept the heinous instrument of death in place and Hannah from any further harm.

I turned back, and the moment my gaze landed on the table, my breath hitched in my chest. The blade of a spear punctured Raven's chest running straight through her from behind. The tip glistened with the blood from her overtaxed heart. The light in her eyes faded and within a blink, her spirit peeled away from her dead form and stood, turning toward me with both sorrow and relief painted on her beautiful features.

I couldn't hold the fury that overtook me. The power let loose, rolling across the room like a bulldozer bent on destruction. I'm not sure if the man knew what hit him, because one second he was standing next to the table with a smug smile, and the next he was flying through the air. With murderous intent, I yanked the pendulum blade from its housing and sent it spinning in the same direction.

With a sickening thud, it split the bastard right in half.

I didn't know if there were other vehicles of torture or booby traps left to trip, but I didn't care. I ran towards my daughter, willing the chains holding her in place to unlatch and I was there to catch her falling form.

My thoughts were jumbled with the shock of Raven's death, but I was with it enough to grip the tube in my fist, intending to rip it out of my daughter. At the last minute, I paused, taking a second to collect my wits. This tube was embedded in her carotid artery. If I yanked it out, she would bleed out in minutes.

"Fuck," I whispered, knowing just how screwed I was. The flow had slowed, but now I had air bubbles in the tube and the change in position made the danger of an air bubble getting into her veins just as horrifying as her bleeding out.

"Don't pull it out," Raven's ghost said as she crouched next to me. "She'll bleed to death."

I stared at her and then dropped my gaze to Hannah, searching for life in her limp form. Her chest rose and fell in shallow breaths, and I closed my eyes, bowing my head in a little prayer to spare her.

When I raised my head, I asked Raven, "Are there any other traps?"

Her eyebrows arched in that cute way I loved, and the sharp pain of loss hit, tightening my chest. "You're a ghost, hon, you can hear my voice like when we go to Paradise Cove," I added, forcing my lips to twist into a small smile. "Traps?" I asked again, twirling my finger indicating the room, reminding her of my original question.

She shook her head. "Not that I know of."

I had no idea how to ensure there were no more boxes of snakes waiting to fall from the ceiling, or another Claymore Mine waiting to detonate.

She glanced over her shoulder, and I followed her gaze to the other ghost now occupying the room. He backed away from his impaled dead body and spun like he was going to run, but something near the door stopped him. The panicked deer-in-the-headlights look on his face pushed my attention to the doorway.

My stomach dropped at the sight of Steve standing there. My breath locked in my chest, and I closed my eyes against the sudden swell of tears. I lost two people I loved today and the child in my arms just couldn't die. Not now.

A hand landed on my shoulder. The physical weight of it pulled my eyes up, and they met Steve's pained gaze. Before the words could come out, Valerie slid to her knees next to me and reached for Hannah. It took my brain a few seconds to catch up, and then I willingly released my daughter into her care.

I stood, staring at Steve. "You're okay?" I asked, and it came out bastardized as usual, but Steve's gaze was locked on the table displaying Raven's dead form.

"Jesus," he whispered before looking back at me with a nod. "Yes. Valerie got there just in time."

As if on cue, CJ stepped into the room, his gaze surveying the damage before landing on Valerie. Seeing her work on my daughter smoothed some of the worry lines on his forehead before his gaze raised to mine. Sadness and fury lived in his irises when they met mine. We both knew who orchestrated this, and I turned towards the ghost on the other side of the room.

"How many of you does Lucifer have working for him?" I snarled.

His gaze snapped to mine, scrunching in fear and anger.

"Fuck you," he said.

I didn't know how to hurt a ghost, but CJ did, and a stream of angel fire crossed the expanse, wrapping around the ghost like a lasso. He screamed as CJ controlled the burn of it.

"He's going to keep crossing off names until there's nothing left. There are plenty of mercenaries willing to take the job with what he's paying."

CJ stepped closer and twisted his fist. The ghost screamed.

"What is he doing with the blood?" I asked.

He laughed. "I have no idea what he's doing with it. He just said to make the deaths look like vampires, and to send him the blood." He waved at the room. "This town was the only one that had different instructions. It was supposed to be last, but I like to be systematic…" He trailed off, his glance bouncing between CJ and me.

"You killed my wife," I said, trying to keep the crushing truth from knocking me to my knees.

He grinned like a true psycho. "I've never stuffed someone with rocks before. It was actually fun."

Before I could react, the angel fire spread, consuming the spiteful bastard. I couldn't help the momentary satisfaction that crept into me. His agonizing screams quenched the vengeance thrumming in my soul, but deep down, I knew it wasn't enough.

Lucifer had to pay for this, one way or another.

When there was nothing left of the ghost, I glanced at my wife.

Heaven was waiting for her, but I didn't want to let her go. I wanted her to stay with me until Hannah was all grown up and I was ready to join her. I wanted a lifetime with her, not a meager blink in time.

Hannah's whine of pain whipped my head in her direction. All the muscles in her small form stood out in stark relief against the light that traveled over every inch of her. Valerie had removed the tube and the gaping wound in her throat stitched up in seconds, leaving only a smear of blood against her perfect skin where the slash had been.

She remained pale, but her breathing steadied, and Valerie looked up at me.

"She may need a transfusion, even with the healing mojo," she said, eyeing the jug of blood.

Unable to trust my voice, I signed, "Thank you."

She sent me a nod, and I met Steve's sad expression. He pulled me into a hug, and I couldn't speak. The last time he hugged me like this was in high school, and I didn't want my mind to go there. That entire nightmare brought Raven into my life.

I broke free and turned, crossing to Raven's body even as her ghost trailed next to me. I felt the cool warmth of her hand on my arm, but I ignored the ghost for a moment. Instead, I focused on the woman who had shared my life for the past eleven years. Tears blurred my vision, and I blinked them away. Gently, I pushed her hair out of her face, and pulled the tape off her mouth before I leaned over and pressed my lips to her cold ones. My hand landed on her abdomen, and I froze at the hard relief map under my palm. Rocks jutted into her skin from the inside and I turned to her ghost, searching her pained expression.

"I'm so sorry, sweetheart," I whispered, and she shook her head.

"I don't want you to remember me like this," she said, and tried to pull me away from her stuffed form.

I sent her a sad smile and blinked away the layer of tears that had formed. "It's a little too late for that, babe."

She knew enough about my nightmares. She knew it was the vision of my parents' death that haunted my thoughts, and not all the happy memories before those horrifying moments. This was just one more that would overshadow all the good we had shared.

I closed my eyes and turned from her body, letting the hands that wrapped around me lead me out of the death room and into the dark night. Strobes of red and blue descended as I sat on the curb with what was left of my family.

Chapter 17

THE CHIEF OF THE York Police department, Duke Gallagher, corralled both Steve and me in an empty waiting room as soon as my daughter was settled in the ICU.

"What the hell did you think you were doing?" he barked pointing at me.

"We..." Steve began, and Chief Gallagher glared, silencing him.

I pulled out the deputy papers that O'Keefe had instituted and handed them to him. He glanced at the orders and then back at me. "He had my wife and daughter. I wasn't going to stop until I found them," I signed. He followed my hand signals and then met my gaze.

"When you became personally involved in the case, you should have stepped down." He shook the papers at me. "The perp had your family, and while I get it, you still should have let us do our job."

My jaw tightened. "O'Keefe and those two rookies were dead when we got there, and that psycho had the place wired with traps," I signed, my hands moving faster as the frustration built. "If I had left it to the police, more people would be dead, including my daughter."

"You don't know that," he growled, and I stepped closer to him.

Steve grabbed my arm, holding me back and the warning in his gaze came through. This wasn't O'Keefe, and revealing what our family could do was not a wise move.

I let my tightly coiled muscles relax and dropped my gaze to the ground.

"What the hell happened?" he asked, but this time it was softer.

"He had a claymore mine set up for anyone who came in the second door."

Chief Gallagher's eyebrows rose.

"I guess it backfired." I knew how unlikely that scenario was, but the force that I used to launch him into the wall was consistent with a bomb of some sort.

"What about the snakes?"

I huffed a laugh. "I hate snakes," I signed.

"So, they were alive?"

I traded a glance with Steve and shrugged.

"Neither of you were bitten, right?"

We both shook our heads.

"Do you know what those were?"

I shook my head.

"Those were death adders, one of the deadliest snakes in the fucking world, and there were at least twenty of them. How the hell did you not get bitten?"

"Just lucky, I guess," I signed.

His lips thinned, and he glanced at the preliminary reports coming in on his blackberry. The crease between his eyes deepened, and he glanced at me as the words on his screen echoed in his head.

"He videotaped it?" I said and signed at the same time.

The chief's gaze narrowed as much as my eyes had widened.

"How did you know that?"

"I can read upside down," I signed, hoping to appease his curiosity. "He videotaped the whole thing?" I asked, paling at the thought.

The Chief didn't answer, but the suspicion in his gaze chilled me. "I expect you to stay in town until this case is closed." He pointed at me and headed towards the door.

I glanced at Steve, but he was staring after Chief Gallagher. When I started towards the door intending to check on Hannah, Steve's hand landed on my arm, and I stopped.

"Why would he tape it?" He turned his gaze to mine.

I shrugged. I had no fucking idea.

"I'm serious."

"I don't have a clue. I need to go see my daughter," I signed, and didn't wait for him to continue, instead, I crossed from the waiting room to the nurse's desk. Steve followed.

He cleared his throat. "Can you tell us which room Hannah Ryan is in?" he asked.

"Only family is allowed in the ICU," the nurse said without looking up.

I banged my palm on the counter and when she looked up, I signed, "I am her father."

"He is Hannah's father," Steve translated, and I flipped open my wallet, showing her my driver's license.

"Oh, I'm sorry, she's in Room 57. Down the hall that way," she said, pointing to her left, after she studied the picture on the license.

"Thank you," I signed and headed down the hall.

Hannah looked so small in the hospital bed, and I slid into the seat next to her, taking her tiny hand in mine.

"She's going to be okay," Steve said and gave my shoulder a pat.

I glanced up at him with a nod. I knew from all my experiences with the healing mojo that she would be okay, but it might take some time. After all, Jennifer had taken over a week from the time my mother infused her to when she woke up.

The machines continued to monitor her vitals, and I scanned all the equipment in the room wondering why she was in intensive care. I glanced at Steve like he could enlighten me, but he was studying the equipment with the same puzzlement I had.

The doctor stepped into the room.

"Mr. Ryan, how are you holding up?"

"Okay, considering," I signed, keeping it as simple as possible.

He pulled up a chair at the foot of the bed and looked at the notes on his tablet. "Your daughter is in a coma, and we aren't sure why. We couldn't find any sign of injury; however her blood count is dangerously low." He glanced up at me. "We are concerned she may have internal bleeding and want to do a CT scan to pinpoint any issue."

I signed yes, with a nod of my fist and followed it with a simple, "Ya."

"If we don't find the cause with the CT scan, we would like your permission to do emergency exploratory surgery," he added.

"No," I articulated, with an emphatic shake of my head. A CT scan was not invasive, and I'd allow that just to appease the doctors. But surgery was out of the question.

"Sir," he started, and I could feel the hardness returning to my muscles. I slowed the shake of my head, stopping him.

"The CT scan is okay, but I will not give you authorization to cut her open," I signed, and Steve translated.

"My son said no," Steve added, when the doctor argued again.

The doctor turned towards him, thinking he was a fountain of reason that could sway me.

"I don't think your son understands the critical nature of the problem."

"He understands better than most what's at stake, and if the CT scan shows internal bleeding, we can revisit this conversation."

The doctor sighed and nodded. "A nurse will be in to bring her down in a few minutes."

"Thank you," I signed.

"Do you need me to stay?" Steve asked after the doctor left.

I didn't know how to answer him. I was still numb from the night's events. Our home was destroyed, as was CJ's and Damian's. Captain O'Keefe was dead. My wife was dead. And my daughter was in a coma. The facts of what had happened in the last few days layered on me like a ton of bricks dropped from a bulldozer.

He offered me a smile of commiseration. He knew what it was like to be in my shoes, except he had sat next to Jennifer's battered body trying to make sense of it all. At least I knew my daughter would wake. Eventually.

"Let me ask you an easier question," he said, pausing in order for me to focus on him. "Can I get you some clothes?"

I huffed a laugh. "From where?" I signed.

"I can take a run down to Kittery and get you a couple of things to tide you and Hannah over," he said.

I gave a nod. Having clean clothing on would be a start. Then maybe I'd be able to feel something other than this complete numbness of mind and emotion.

"Jennifer should be here in a little bit. She's helping CJ and Valerie to find temporary housing. We found a place for you and Hannah to stay until you have time to rebuild."

I hadn't been by my house, but I had seen the rubble at CJ's. "Did they ever figure out what caused the explosions?"

He gave me a long look. "They think it was ship to shore missiles," he finally said.

My eyes widened. "Missiles? What the fuck? Does that mean there was more than one person?" My mind went back to the things the assassin's ghost rattled about. They would never stop until all the angel descendants were dead, including us. The way he glanced over my head and out the window unnerved my already frazzled psyche.

"I honestly don't know. Based on the timing of Jennifer's vision and the hardware he had in his van, he had the means and the time to get a boat out there and back. People on the beach said they saw the heat trails but couldn't identify the boat they came from. The Coast Guard found no trace of whoever had done it, either."

I digested the information and gave him a nod. "Just make sure everyone is close together. We are stronger that way," I added as he stood to leave.

"Jeans or shorts?" he asked at the door.

"Both." York could get chilly at night even with the hot days and I wasn't sure how long I'd be sitting at Hannah's bedside in the chill of the hospital room.

He gave me a nod and disappeared through the door.

I focused on the figure I had been ignoring since I walked into the room and offered Raven's ghost a brief semblance of a smile. She stood on the opposite side of the bed with Hannah's hand in hers.

I think the fact I could still see my wife kept the soul-crushing pain at bay.

Chapter 18

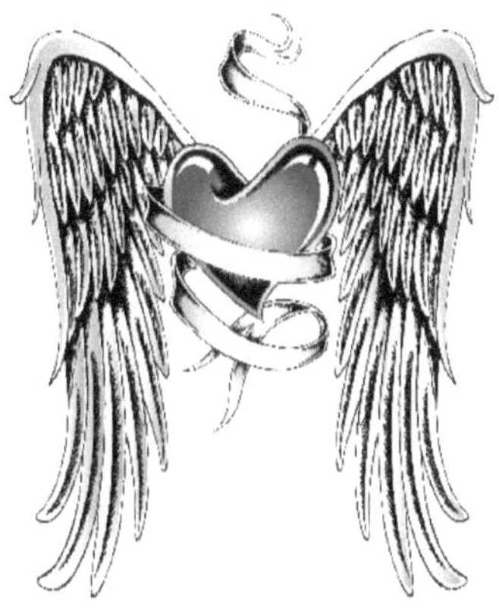

I WASN'T VERY GOOD at praying, but I closed my eyes and bowed my head. Before I could form any words, the door swung open. I glanced up at a face I hadn't seen before, and behind him stood Valerie.

"What's up?" I signed, looking at my sister-in-law and not the doctor who had preceded her into the room.

"Dr. Phillips has a proposal for you," she said. Her mind was projecting static, so I didn't really know what was coming.

"As you know, your wife was listed as an organ donor. Unfortunately, most of her organs were damaged beyond use; however, there were a few parts that were salvageable."

I crossed my arms, pressing my lips together at the way he referred to my wife, as if she were a used car.

He cleared his throat and offered me a nervous smile. "We would like your permission to send her eyes to John's Hopkins for a transplant."

I glanced at Raven's ghost and she smiled, nodding. If her death could result in someone else living a better life, she was all for it, and my skeptical irritation eased. I turned my gaze back to Dr. Phillips and gave him a nod.

"She would want that," I signed. Valerie translated.

He handed me one of the two papers in his hand, and I signed on the dotted line where he indicated.

When I handed that back, he licked his lips and glanced at Valerie.

"Did you know Raven's blood type matches yours?" Valerie asked, and I gave her a nod. That I knew, but I had no idea where they were going with the question.

"Were you aware that Mr. Williams had you on a transplant list?"

My eyebrows rose, and I glanced between Valerie and Dr. Phillips. "That was a long time ago, and they said it wasn't possible," I signed, as Valerie translated.

Dr. Phillips offered me a soft smile. "There have been significant advances in this area, and I'd like to offer you the option, especially since we have a viable tongue that matches your blood type."

I blinked at the statement and when the facts came together all at once, I balked.

"Are you asking me if I want my wife's tongue transplanted into my mouth?" The shock of his offer left me stunned, and when he nodded, I looked at Valerie. "And you're on board with this?"

"You know she would have done anything to make you whole again," Valerie said.

I gave a sarcastic laugh and sat back in the chair, staring at the two of them, unsure of how to react. "I'll never be whole again," I finally signed, irritated at the suggestion.

"Tom," Raven's ghost interrupted, and I looked square at her. "Let me do this for you. Please," she whispered.

"Why should I?" I asked the ghost.

"If you do this, I will always be a part of you."

"You already are."

She cocked her head and leveled her 'don't be an ass' look.

I closed my eyes and laid my forehead on the side of the bed; taking a few breaths so the burning tears would stay at the back of my throat and not cascade down my face. Raven's rationale hit home, and my heart ached for her.

Valerie came closer and crouched down so I could see her. "Tom, this is an opportunity to actually speak to your daughter."

I turned my head and stared at her. "I speak to her now," I said aloud. She heard the thought, and the bastardized sounds. "What makes you think she doesn't understand me?" I added, trying to keep the irritation from overwhelming me.

"She's going to need you, Tom," she whispered. "And if you don't take this opportunity, they will give it to someone else. I have a feeling Raven would rather have you find some benefit from her' loss than some stranger." She looked directly at the spot where Raven stood, and I followed her glance.

Raven was nodding.

I sat up and sniffled, still not sure I should accept the offer. "How long is the procedure?"

"The surgery takes between four and six hours, depending on factors such as how damaged the nerve and muscles are in your mouth," Dr. Phillips answered. "And the hospital stay afterwards can range between seven to ten days, depending on how you react to the transplant."

"Could I stay in here with Hannah?" I asked, looking between the doctor and Valerie.

"Unfortunately, that is not an option," Dr. Phillips said. "This is the children's wing. Adult patients are not allowed to stay here," he added, clarifying the rules.

"Then, no." It was a simple choice for me. I had to be here when my daughter woke, even if it meant giving up the possibility of normal speech.

"We will take turns watching over Hannah for you, and once you are out of danger of infection, we can make sure you can spend your days here instead of in a hospital room in the adult wing. If Hannah wakes up, we can take her home with us until you are released. Would that change your mind?" Valerie said. I knew she wanted this for me, the same way Raven did, but I couldn't leave Hannah unattended even for a minute.

"You and CJ have a newborn. You can't be here twenty-four-seven," I signed, digging in on my argument.

"True, but it isn't just the two of us. We have Steve and Jennifer and Damian and Naomi, so between the six of us, we have this covered. She will not be left alone at all."

"Tom," Raven's ghost interjected, pulling my attention to her. "Don't be such a stubborn ass. Take the opportunity," she added, and her hands found her hips. Even in ghostly form, she knew how to project her irritation.

You really want me to do this? I silently asked, and she nodded. *Then you have to stay by Hannah's side and let me know when she wakes up, otherwise, I'm not doing it.*

"I promise I will stay by her side," Raven said. "Please take this gift. It's all I have to offer you now," she added, her voice softening just as her eyes pleaded with me. It was a look I could never say no to when she was alive, and as a ghost, the effect magnified.

I looked down at the floor, weighing my options. Leaving Hannah didn't sit well with me at all, but neither did disappointing Raven.

"You promise she won't ever be alone," I signed, looking up at Valerie.

"Yes. I promise. Someone will always be by her side, keeping her safe while you are in surgery and recovering." She spelled it out for me, so nothing was left to chance, and I sighed.

"If she wakes up, you have to let me know immediately, and I need to be brought here to her side, so she knows I'm okay. All right?"

Valerie translated for the doctor and they both nodded ascent.

"Absolutely," Valerie said.

I leaned over and whispered in Hannah's ear. "I promise I'll be back." My words were a jumble of sounds, and I kissed her slack cheek before following the doctor out of the children's ICU and into the pre-surgical unit for a quick physical and blood work.

Two hours later, I was being prepped for surgery and Valerie came into the room.

"I have a feeling your recovery will be faster than normal," she said and sent me a wink, which meant I'd have to endure the pain that came with her healing mojo once the operation was finished.

"Am I doing the right thing?" I signed, meeting her gaze as the nerves started in earnest.

Valerie nodded. "You heard what she said. She wants this, and deep down, so do you." She gave my arm a squeeze and left just as the anesthesiologist stepped into the room to administer the anesthesia into my intravenous line.

I was told to count backwards from one hundred. I think I got to ninety-seven before everything went black.

Chapter 19

I SHIVERED AND TRIED to swallow, but my mouth was so pasty it just produced a dry hack instead. Someone was talking to me, and I attempted to lift my eyelids, but they were so heavy that all I got was a dose of light and then I let them drop again.

The world sounded like I was underwater, and I drifted, letting the flow take me down.

Again, I tried to swallow, and something stuck to the roof of my mouth. I opened my jaws to dislodge whatever it was, and something cold ran over my lips. I forced my eyes open and looked into a nurse's hazel eyes.

Her mouth was moving, but I was still underwater, so it was all garbled. Until the thing stuck to the roof of my mouth moved and something scraped my lips. I blinked, and her words came into clear focus.

"Mr. Ryan, can you hear me?"

I nodded, distracted by the colored hue surrounding her. The flow of the pinks, greens and oranges mesmerized me as much as her calm voice did .

"You are in the recovery room and as soon as the doctor comes in to check on you, we will move you to the intensive care unit for the night."

"Intensive care?" My hoarse whisper was more pronounced than I remembered, and the nurse put her finger on my lips.

"Don't try to talk. It will aggravate the swelling in your tongue." She rubbed another ice chip on my lips. "From what I heard, you did really well," she added with a smile.

I was still foggy on where I was, so I just let it go and enjoyed the cool wetness of the ice chips being rubbed on my lips.

When the doctor entered the room, the light surrounding him pulsed with yellow, red, and silver strands. He scanned the tablet in his hands and then met my gaze.

"The surgery was quicker than I anticipated, and the blood flow into the new tongue seemed adequate in the operating room. I will just want to check it again to validate it is still circulating. We will have to monitor the swelling through the night, and if all goes well, we can take the oxygen tubes out tomorrow."

I reached up, feeling the tube under my nose with my finger before signing, "Do you know if my daughter has woken yet?"

He offered me a wry smile, and the red bloomed around him. "Your sister-in-law said that would be the first thing you asked, and no, she is still in a coma."

The colors surrounding both him and the nurse distracted me, and I blinked, trying to focus on the people, not the surrounding flares. "I think I'm still out of it," I signed. "I'm seeing a lot of colors."

"Well, you are on some hefty pain medicine and some people have mild hallucinations from the anesthesia. It is nothing to worry about." He put the tablet down and leaned closer, pulling what looked like a popsicle stick from his pocket. "Can you open your mouth wide for me?" he asked.

I did as he said, but then Valerie stepped into the room and the white light radiating from her was blinding and I squinted, trying to avert my gaze. She stopped short and through the light surrounding her; I saw her wide-eyed surprise.

"Things look good," Dr. Phillips stood and gave me a nod. He turned to the nurse. "He can be moved as soon as his vision clears." He turned and gave Valerie an encouraging nod. "I don't think there is anything more for me to do here. I'll write up the instructions for the ICU and the daily checks after. If signs of rejection present, call me." He shook her hand and left the little fabric enclosed room.

Valerie approached, and the nurse excused herself. When they were out of earshot, Valerie leaned over and placed a kiss on my forehead, and my mouth immediately felt like it was on fire. I clamped my eyes shut against the knitting agony. Instead, I focused on taking long, slow breaths while the pain eclipsed everything else.

When it finally receded into that annoying pins and needles sensation, I opened my eyes and stared at Valerie. The silver-white surrounding her now flowed with all the colors of the rainbow. It was beautiful. She smiled at me.

"You can see auras now?"

My gaze snapped away from the colors surrounding her to her eyes.

"Is that what they are?" I asked in a nearly perfect diction. The clarity made my chest draw tight. The only time I spoke clearly was when someone was a ghost.

"I'm not dead, Tom," she said, reading my mind as easily as CJ did.

I reached up and tentatively touched the muscle in my mouth. The sensation was odd after not having most of my tongue for twenty years. I felt the pressure of my fingers and then swiped the back of my teeth, feeling the smooth enamel for the first time since I was nine years old.

"Holy shit," I said, my voice raspy from surgery, but intact except for a slight lisp with the letter 's'.

"You have a lovely voice," she said and offered me a smile. "But you have to play along." She twirled her finger around and I got her reference, nodding.

"Your aura is stunning," I said, and pressed my lips together against a smirk at the 'th' sound instead of 's' when I said stunning. CJ and I would make a fine pair. His stutter and my newly formed lisp would be the center of fun at our next Thanksgiving feast.

Valerie allowed a smirk in response. "I promise not to make fun of you," she said, but I could tell it was total bullshit. Especially since I gave CJ such a hard time with his stutter. "Wait 'til you see your aura. Raven said yours was the most beautiful one she had ever seen."

Just the reference to my wife carved a pain in my chest and I pressed my lips together, closing my eyes against the sudden wetness that blurred my vision. I turned my head away so Valerie wouldn't see the tears, but the chair scraped against the floor anyway, and her hand squeezed my shoulder.

I preferred to be numb than the emotional rollercoaster the medicine seemed to brush me with. I took a breath and turned back to Valerie.

"Thank you," I signed, blinking the wetness from my eyes.

She pressed her lips together. "If I had my choice, she would have made it and you'd still be mute." Her eyes swelled with tears, and I took her hand, squeezing.

"Me, too." I whispered and pulled my hand away. "How's Alex?" I asked, hoping for some sort of distraction from the pain wrapping around Valerie. Otherwise, I'd drown in it.

She wiped her cheeks. "He seems like such a happy baby," she said. "Kind of like the way Grace was, you know?"

I nodded. Grace was a joy. Even as a newborn she exhibited awareness of her surroundings and she rarely fussed unless she was wet or hungry. The rest of the time, she had been content just to observe.

"And Grace doesn't want to leave him alone. Talk about a mother hen," she said and rolled her eyes.

I couldn't help but smile. The interaction in the hospital room gave me a hint of what she was talking about. If Hannah had been awake, I am sure she would dote on the newborn as well. She loved playing mommy with her dolls, so I'd imagine Grace would have some competition there.

"As tiring as it is, she has been quite the little helper," she said, and my smile faded.

I glanced at her, all of her, and then returned my gaze to her face. She gave birth three days ago, and she didn't look like it at all. "How are you holding up with all this?"

Valerie gave me a shrug. "I am still pretty numb. Giving birth and then all this, it's been quite taxing." She offered me a small smile. "Truth is, the only thing keeping me together is Alex." She looked down at her hands before she returned my gaze. "CJ wants to start closing portals again."

I nodded. If I had my druthers, I'd be out doing that right now, but I also knew Hannah was still on Lucifer's hit list and I wasn't leaving that to chance. I'm sure the devil was livid with how his hired hand screwed up the grand plan by being systematic instead of following orders.

I wondered what kind of torture chamber that bastard was in right now.

I fancied one where he was continuously stuffed with bloodstone until he split wide open.

The chair scraped again, and I glanced at Valerie. The agitation in her aura told me more than her wide eyes and I toned down my thoughts, signing the symbol for sorry.

"Is it bad that I hope he suffers her pain a thousandfold?"

I reached for her hand, cradling it, letting her express her feelings instead of focusing on my misery and I shook my head because I wished the same, but magnified by a million. She'd lost her closest friend, and her hurt wavered between manageable and overwhelming; as long as I focused on her feelings, I could pretend mine didn't exist.

"Was this your idea?" I whispered and pointed at my mouth. York Hospital was not known for their revolutionary technology, but Valerie had contacts from her days at medical school at Harvard.

She nodded. "When they told me they were harvesting her eyes for a donor down at John's Hopkins, I asked if her tongue was viable for a transplant. When they said yes, I called Dr. Phillips. He's done this a couple of times down in Boston, so I thought it would be worth his while to take a trip up here." She kept eye contact with me while she explained. "Raven and I talked about it. She said if she died before you, she wanted me to make sure you got the voice you were meant to have," she said and huffed a little laugh. "The conversation went totally off track when she mentioned her tongue, but in the end, she said she was serious, and I agreed."

I just stared at her wondering how that conversation really went. How would Raven even know how to approach the subject?

"Raven was direct when a thought entered her head, you know that," she said, reading my thoughts again.

I gave her a huff of a laugh in response, nodding. "That she was," I signed to save my voice.

"And you were still on that list, so it lifted a lot of red tape," she added with a smile.

The curtain shuffled, and the nurse peeked her head in. "How are we doing?"

I gave her a thumbs up and she smiled through her now yellow-orange glow. I was going to have to get used to ignoring the colors and seeing the people inside the aura.

"Actually, you should pay attention to them, at least on a cursory glance," Valerie said, pulling my gaze to her. "Raven gave me a sheet of what the colors mean and while I used to think it was hogwash, I eventually came around when I saw her father's aura through her eyes."

She shivered in the seat, and I raised my eyebrows, waiting for her to continue.

"I'd give it to you, but it's under all that rubble," she continued. "I'm sure we can look it up online, but she told me to watch out for anyone showing predominately dark brown or black auras. Those are trouble," she said. "The color rationale is quite intriguing, and she said it was pretty accurate."

"Good to know," I said aloud.

She glanced at her watch. "I need to get back. Steve is with Hannah while I came here. I still have an hour before CJ brings Alex in."

"Thank you," I whispered, and she gave me a pat on the shoulder, leaving me to the mercy of the happy nursing staff. I focused on faces while letting the colors swirl in my peripheral vision.

The swelling in my tongue had reduced significantly, and the ICU staff wasn't sure what to make of me, but when I was safely tucked into the bed, they gave me another dose of pain medicine. I didn't make a fuss, even though I didn't need any medication after Valerie's visit. I figured it would

dope me up enough to allow me to get some much-
needed sleep.

Chapter 20

I STUMPED THE DOCTORS the next day when they examined me. The lack of swelling and the range of movement I had amazed them, and the healing around the stitches was more advanced than they'd expected.

Dr. Phillips left a detailed set of instructions that outlined the conditions for release. I met every one, and they removed the oxygen tubes, which burned all the way up my throat and through my nose. Once they were out, I was able to breathe through my mouth and my nose with no issue.

They let me have a smoothie to gauge how well I could swallow food, and I let the cold drink drench my tongue, fully tasting a meal for the first time in twenty years. It was exhilarating, and I wanted more.

"Can I have pancakes?" I asked as the ICU doctor re-read the notes left behind.

He looked up at me. "I'm not sure," he said, and the confusion clouding his aura pulsed. "According to the notes, you are presenting better than day seven, but if I'm reading this right, you're only on day one, right?"

"I've always been a fast healer," I said softly and shrugged, trying to pass this off as normal, but he didn't take the bait.

"I think I should give Dr. Phillips a call to confirm, because according to his list, you are ready for a full release."

"Maybe you should touch base with Dr. Ryan first. Wasn't she the one who brought him in for the surgery?" I asked, trying to lead him down the right path for subterfuge.

He gave me a nod and started out of the room.

"Pancakes?" I asked before he was out of earshot. He turned, contemplating, before he gave me a single nod.

I lifted the phone and put in an order for pancakes with syrup. I almost asked for Nutella because I always wondered what that tasted like. It wasn't something I had when I was young, so I really had no clue.

I stretched out on the bed, flipping through the television channels waiting for either my meal or the doctor to come back. As luck would have it, my meal came first, and I didn't wait for permission. I drenched the short stack in syrup and took a bite.

The sugary substance tasted glorious, and I was so preoccupied with enjoying the full taste of food, I didn't even notice the visitor in the doorway.

"Feeling better I see," Gallagher's rough voice pulled my attention from my food and I met his blatant stare. His aura pulsed a dark blue and deep green and I wished like hell I had that guide, because his eyes were piercing.

"Is Hannah awake?" I said around the mouthful of food.

"Talking already?" he asked, raising an eyebrow.

I nodded and wiped my mouth. "Faster than anyone expected," I said, and his lips pursed.

"Well, I just came by to see for myself. I'll be on my way," he said, and turned before I could say anything more.

The doctor scooted by him in the doorway, giving the chief a smile before focusing on me. "With how well you're doing, we can let you get out of here." He grinned. "I've taken the liberty to schedule a couple of outpatient appointments for you. We want to touch base daily to make sure your body continues to accept the transplant. Here's a list of things to look out for; if you experience any of those, immediately return." He handed me a list and a prescription bottle. "Antibiotics," he said to my raised eyebrow. "Twice a day until they are gone to prevent infection."

"Okay," I said and took the last bite of pancakes, soaking up the rest of the syrup before I stuffed it in my mouth.

"Your clothing is hanging on the back of the door over there and there are towels in the cabinet if you want to take a quick shower. Otherwise, you are officially released."

"I think I'll take you up on that shower," I said. I felt utterly grimy from the surgery.

"I'll send the nurse to get you in..." He looked at his watch. "Twenty minutes."

I gave him a nod and climbed out of the bed, heading for that shower. My clothes felt fresh compared to the hospital gown and when I wiped away the steam to get a clue as to what my hair looked like, my aura sparkled back at me, and I stared at the myriad of colors. Interwoven in the rich rainbow surrounding me was gold, silver and pure white, like an intricate braid. It certainly was unique from the other auras I had seen since I woke from surgery, and there wasn't a hint of brown or black to be found.

My gaze shifted to my eyes, and my wonder sobered. The only reason I was seeing auras was because a part of my wife's tongue was sewn into my mouth. The joy of speaking and tasting fell flat with the surfacing of the only reason I was enjoying myself.

My heart twisted in my chest, and I ran my hands through my hair, making it presentable before I stepped back into the room.

A young nurse waited with a wheelchair.

"Really?" I gestured towards the chair.

"Standard protocol," she said with a sweet smile.

"I would rather not," I said, my voice much smoother than it had been when I left the recovery room yesterday. "Besides, I'm going to the children's ICU where my daughter is. She's in a coma."

Her gaze softened. "I can bring you there," she said, still quoting procedure in her head.

I knew it wasn't a battle that I would win, and arguing would only waste time, so I deposited my ass in the chair and let her roll me to Hannah's room.

At the door, I stood and turned. "Thanks for the ride," I said, and she gave me a nod. Across the hall, an officer lingered at the nursing station, his aura predominately red with fleeting strands of blue slowly twisting with red strands. I turned back to the cracked door, pushing it open.

Naomi glanced up from the book she held and smiled. Her aura was intriguing, it held gold and silver along with strands of blue and yellow and a very light braided strand of gray and white. I imagine that might be the tiger strand. I wondered if this was what her aura looked like when she was a vampire.

I shook the thought from my head and glanced at Hannah. Her aura was like mine, except it was absent the gold and silver braid. Hers was just a sparkling rainbow, exactly what I envisioned for my three-year-old princess.

"That was fast," she said, and I glanced at the clock. It was just about thirty hours from when I had been escorted to surgery and I shrugged.

"I owe that to Valerie," I said. My gaze traveled across the space to where Raven's ghost sat. "And my wife," I added, giving her a nod of acknowledgement. "Any change?"

"No," she said while shaking her head. "They've been pressuring us to get permission to do exploratory surgery, but we've all held them at bay. The CT scan showed nothing."

"Thank you for keeping watch," I said, and she stood, crossing and giving me a quick hug.

"You know, it wasn't a problem. You've been there for all of us so many times. It was refreshing to be the one to help," she said as she pulled away. "I have to admit, it is strange hearing you talk. I've only heard you when we were at Paradise Cove."

"Trust me, it is just as strange being able to talk." The lisp presented itself and I felt the heat in my cheeks, but today it was a lot less prevalent than yesterday, so maybe there was hope.

"I'm going to get going. Damian and CJ are sifting through the rubble, trying to see if there's anything to salvage. I think Steve and Jennifer are doing the same at your place. If you need us, just yell."

I would have to remember to thank them. I would have let the pile sit until Hannah woke up, and who knows how many more days that would be. "Thanks. I'll be here if anyone wants a break," I said, and she nodded, heading out of the room.

I took a seat next to my daughter and looked at Raven's ghost. She had a hint of an aura, but it was faded. The colors muted in a way that tightened my throat.

"Did you know I'd be able to see auras?" I asked. I was amused by this new manifestation, and I wondered what other surprises I'd have to deal with because of this lovely transplant.

The right side of Raven's lips tilted into a half smile. "I had hoped," she said.

I let a small chuckle out. "Does this mean you'll be with me from now on?" I asked. A sliver of hope bloomed in my heart, but it quickly disappeared, along with Raven's smile.

She slowly shook her head. My heart squeezed, and I leaned back in the chair, sobering at the thought of not seeing her again.

"I'm waiting to say goodbye to Hannah." Her eyes held the depth of her sorrow. "You know I can't stay."

As much as I wanted her to, I knew what happened to ghosts who overstayed their welcome. Any goodness they possessed faded until they were bitter, angry entities bent on destroying everything around them.

My father was the exception.

He called it penance, but I'm not so sure. I think he just returned to his true self.

A guardian angel of sorts, albeit a kick-ass guardian angel, and he'd be there to welcome Raven into heaven.

Chapter 21

THE NEXT MORNING, CHIEF Gallagher stepped into the room with an armed officer and his aura pulsed erratically with an array of color, including a light brown, which made me pay attention based on what Valerie had said.

"Tom, I'm going to need you to come down to the station with us," he said with such caution that I stiffened in the seat.

"Why?" I said, wishing Steve hadn't gone to the hotel to catch some sleep after his quick visit last night.

He cleared his throat, studying me for a moment, especially with how clear my voice was today. "We have some questions, and I don't think this is the right environment for us to ask them."

I leaned back in the seat, staring at him, trying to pull information from his mind, but all I kept getting from him was raw anger, and I was too damned tired to push. The antibiotics had given me a bout of heartburn and I hadn't slept much because of that.

"If I refuse?" I waited to see what would come next.

He shifted and reached into his jacket, pulling out a sheet of paper. "We don't want to cause a scene here," he said, and handed me the paper.

I opened it and stared at the first line. It was a warrant for my arrest, and I glanced up at him in complete confusion.

"I don't understand?" I said, and the lisp presented like it had yesterday. I was dumbfounded enough to sign as well.

"We can discuss this down at the station," he said, and his hand fell onto his service revolver.

I glanced at Raven's ghost and then at my daughter. From everything Steve told me, a warrant for arrest meant they had enough evidence for probable cause, and I just nodded and stood.

When he pulled the handcuffs out of his pocket, I gave him a look and said, "Really?"

"Standard procedure," he said.

I put the arrest warrant on the table and put my hands out in front of me so he could cuff me. "I have a post-surgical appointment at noon. Is that going to be a problem?" I asked, glancing at the clock. It was barely seven.

"I'm afraid you will have to turn around," he said, eyeing me and ignoring my question. I closed my eyes against the irritation, turning without anymore protest. "You might want to cancel that appointment," he added as he clamped the cuffs tighter than necessary.

I sent the current situation out to CJ, Damian, and Steve while the Chief read me my rights. When he asked if I understood them, I nodded. Being paraded through the hospital in police custody made the day that much worse. The glares I received from the nursing staff were enough to ruffle my feathers, but I had been through worse, and I kept my eyes straight ahead, with my head up.

By the time we got to the police station, CJ, Damian, and Steve were leaning on the back of my SUV, waiting for me.

"Who's with Hannah?" I asked, my gaze traveling over the three of them.

"Jennifer is," Steve said, and straightened along with CJ and Damian.

Chief Gallagher held up his hand, as they approached. "Go home boys, the only one that I'll allow in the interrogation room is his lawyer."

"That would be me," Steve said, following us into the station. CJ and Damian paused, unsure of whether or not to follow, and Steve stopped at the door. "Go back and make sure the family is looked after."

CJ and I exchanged a glance, and I just shrugged. I didn't know much of anything right now, but I knew the interrogation room was where I'd find out much more than I probably wanted.

They took the cuffs off and pointed at the farthest chair, and Chief Gallagher took a seat across from me, with a folder in front of him. He stared at me, sizing me up—waiting. A couple of minutes passed, and I never broke his inquisitive stare until the door opened and a deputy stepped in with a laptop encased in a plastic bag. I blinked a couple of times and then turned to Steve.

"What are they doing with my laptop?" I asked, and I received a glare in response. Steve wanted me to shut my mouth, but I couldn't help the flurry of questions fighting to spill all over the table. Instead, I pressed my lips together and remained quiet.

Gallagher let a smirk appear. "You thought since you destroyed your own house, we wouldn't bother looking at your office?"

"What the hell are you talking about?" I snapped, mystified at the accusation.

"The feed went from the kill room to your laptop." He spun it around so I could see the screen and I shrank back in the chair at the view of Raven hogtied. The noise of the air gun pumping bloodstone into her couldn't drown her muffled screams. "You're a sick fuck. Recording this shit for posterity?"

"Turn it off," I hissed. I couldn't tear my eyes from the agony reflected in my wife's eyes. My stomach clenched, and I pressed farther back in the chair, fully aware of the last thing I ate now rolling in my stomach, getting ready for a mass exodus.

Steve leaned forward and shut the laptop, glaring at Gallagher.

My chest hurt and my entire form shook. I couldn't shake the imprint that video left on my brain. I stared at the laptop like it was one of the snakes that attacked Steve. I had seen enough horrific things in my life, but that took the prize, and I finally raised my gaze, still unable to draw a sufficient breath.

Gallagher sat with his arms crossed, studying me closely.

"Breathe," Steve said softly, pulling my attention to him. I stared into his sea-blue eyes as the panic started shutting down my lungs. "Breathe," he said again. Slowly, he inhaled and exhaled. "Slow and easy," he said, repeating until I found I was following his breathing pattern and able to draw enough air.

My eyes misted, and I closed them, concentrating on the hot paths that cut across my cheeks. One tear found the corner of my lips and I swiped my tongue out, capturing the salty bead. I drew another slow breath and when I thought I had control; I opened my eyes and met Gallagher's gaze.

"Sorry," I said, but my voice vibrated with the shakes still present in my form.

He didn't seem fazed by my display, but his thoughts centered on wondering if I was genuine or just a phenomenal actor like my father.

He opened the folder, turning a photo around so I could see it. "Is this your boat?"

I looked at the name—Celtic Princess—and nodded. "Yes. Why?"

"It was found on the rocks over at Lobster Cove with this inside." He turned the next photograph my way, and I stared at a long gray cylinder with what looked like a gun trigger on it.

"What the hell is that?" I asked before I picked up the picture.

"A rocket launcher."

My gaze snapped to his, and my jaw dropped open. I turned to Steve, and he took a cursory glance at the photo before returning his sharp gaze to Chief Gallagher.

"Were my client's fingerprints found on it?"

"No." Chief Gallagher said and leaned forward. "But who else could have orchestrated such an elaborate plot to get rid of his wife?"

I stared at him. "You are out of your fucking mind," I said, and then leaned back in my chair, running my hands through my hair. "I can't believe you think I would do that to my wife." I pointed at the computer, utterly disgusted. "Or to my daughter. What do you think I am?"

I was on my feet, staring down at the Chief.

"I think you're every bit as evil as Ty Ryan was."

"Sit down, Tom," Steve barked, and I glanced at him and pointed at the Chief.

"He thinks I orchestrated all this?"

"Sit down," he said again, and the hardness in his eyes gave me pause. I lowered into the chair slowly. Then he turned that glare in the Chief's direction. "I'll give you props for the theatrics, but you do not have evidence that my son was in cahoots with the killer." His emphasis on the words my son did not go unnoticed by the Chief. "All you have is an elaborate setup designed to make him look guilty."

"Are you in here as his lawyer or his surrogate father?" the Chief asked.

"I'm here because you are as wrong about this as you were about the Windwalker," Steve said.

"What's his motive?" Steve asked after a few moments.

The chief looked down at the file like the evidence would manufacture some sort of concrete motive. "A viable tongue," he said and glanced up from the file.

His tone chilled me, and my mouth dropped open. "I would rather have my wife than be able to talk. What the fuck?" I couldn't help the outburst and Steve shook his head, silencing any further rant.

"Maybe she was going to leave you and take half your fortune. Maybe you were having an affair and wanted her gone, or you found out she was screwing around." He knew he was reaching, but his mind wasn't willing to latch on to any other logical explanation, not without exhausting this one.

"What about blowing up the houses? If what you are insinuating is true, why would he do that to his brother and his business partner? Why would he blow up his own house?" Steve pushed.

"A diversion. And maybe he hates his brother and business partner."

"You are out of your goddamned mind," I said, and received a glare from Steve.

Steve leaned back in the chair. "Chief, Jim was the one who got Tom and his partner messed up in this case. How does that play into your outlandish scenario?"

Gallagher collected the pictures and dropped them on top of the folder, closing it. "Jim mentioned he spoke with Tom and said there was a lot he had to think about. He wanted to keep an eye on him but wouldn't give me any details," he said to Steve, and then looked at me. "Why would my best detective want to keep an eye on you?"

I kept my mouth shut and crossed my arms, shrugging.

"None of this makes sense," Steve said. "You have seen Tom and Raven together, Chief."

"Appearances can be deceiving." Chief Gallagher leveled a glare at Steve and then it turned on me. "What are you hiding?"

"Nothing," I said. "I was working with Captain O'Keefe to help catch this psycho before the bastard got to our town." That earned a glare from Steve. Keeping silent was nearly impossible now that I could speak, especially with such bullshit being thrown in my direction.

Gallagher stopped pussyfooting around and went the direct route. "Were you involved in the abduction and murder of your wife?" he asked.

"No." I shook my head and out of habit, added the hand sign for no.

"Were you involved in blowing up your brother's home?"

"No."

"Were you involved in blowing up your partner's house?"

"No."

"Were you involved in blowing up your own home?"

"No."

The Chief's aura calmed from violent pulsing to a slower calmer flow, and he rubbed his face before he pushed the off button on the recording.

"Whose blood is in the snake room?" he asked looking between Steve and me.

I pointed at Steve before he could stop me.

Gallagher sighed. "I thought you said neither of you got bit?" Instead of waiting for an answer, he barreled ahead. "How did half a gallon of blood that matches your daughter's get into that jug? And how the hell can you talk so fluidly the day after a fucking tongue transplant?"

Neither of those questions was easy to answer, because giving up Valerie as a miracle healer wasn't something I was willing to do. I glanced at Steve for help and all I got was a miniscule shake of his head.

"Look. Either you are the best fucking actor on the planet, or your father here is right. Someone is trying damned hard to set you up. I've got a shit ton of questions that I don't have any logical answers to, and there is zero on that video that would explain any of this." He ran his hand over the top of his buzz cut and sighed.

I glanced at the laptop. "Where does that end?" I asked and pointed.

"When you tripped the explosion." He stared at me, expecting a different answer than I gave earlier and I dropped my gaze to the table. "You are hiding something, aren't you boy? And if it isn't your involvement in this case, what the hell is it?"

"Are we being observed?" Steve asked, looking at the one-way mirror behind the Chief.

"No," both the Chief and I said at the same time and his eyebrows creased.

"How the hell do you know that?"

"Because he is psychic," Steve answered.

"Don't bullshit me."

"I'm not, Duke. Jim came to me because he knew... he knew I had some special abilities, except I don't. Not anymore. I'm the one who sent him to Tom."

"Then you know what we were originally thinking," he said, looking between Steve and me. "Unfortunately, that video changed the entire thought process," he added and laid his hand on the computer. "We now know he was using the snake venom to subdue the victims and a low suction machine to drain the bodies. But I still don't know how your daughter came out of there without a scratch."

"There is an explanation, but it's as out there as vampires," I said. "It pertains to how fast I healed as well."

Chief Gallagher let out a short laugh. "Both Jim and I were nearly convinced that vampires existed," he admitted, and I kept my expression neutral. I didn't want to burst that bubble.

"Where do you want me to start?" I transmitted without speaking.

He blinked and moved his gaze to Steve, unsure of himself. A thin thread of light brown weaved into his aura, and I had to focus on not staring at the hesitation so visible around him.

"Chief Gallagher, this is Tom, and you aren't losing it. I really am talking in your head."

Steve looked between the two of us, and I glanced over at him and shrugged.

"For the love of God, Tom," he said to me with irritation laced into every syllable and then turned to Gallagher. "He's talking to you, isn't he?"

"How?"

"I told you, he's psychic. He can read minds and transmit thoughts."

"Based on what I saw on that video, his daughter should have died. So should both of you. That bomb didn't malfunction. The debris field was in an arc around where he stood." Gallagher pointed at me, still staring at Steve. "The walls, ceiling, everything. He should have been shredded to hell and back. We should have been picking up pieces of him in the parking lot. Instead, he's sitting here without a scratch, and he's got a new tongue

244

out of the deal." He gave me a cursory glance and continued. "According to the preliminary report, the blood on the floor matches the blood on at least a dozen of those viper's teeth. You should be as dead as O'Keefe."

"Would you believe we have a guardian angel?" Steve said, offering a hint of a smile.

"I'd believe just about anything right now," he muttered. "You and I have known each other for a long time," he said to Steve with more of a sigh than a statement. "And I know these kids gave you a run for your money at times." He waved in my direction. "But despite what the evidence suggests, I'm having a hard time putting any other logical explanation together in my mind."

"There isn't anything logical about this, Chief," I said. "Just like there is no logical explanation why I've been able to see ghosts all my life."

He took a great inhalation. "So, do you know why he was killing all these people?"

I stared at him for a few minutes and then gave a slow nod. "Yes."

"Do you know why your wife's death differed from the rest?"

I knew this question was coming, and I bit my lip as a sheen of tears blurred my eyes. I blinked away the tears, unwilling to break down any further than I already had here. "Because I got in the way of his goal."

"Who's goal?"

"Whoever orchestrated all this shit."

Gallagher's face reddened in frustration, and he pulled a couple of sheets from the file, smoothing them out before he handed them to me. "Can you tell me anything about this?"

I glanced at the list. It was similar to the one CJ wrote, except in geographical order, going from northeast to southwest. Names and towns, and it did indeed say we were to be the last of the hit, so in that respect, the ghost was telling us the truth. The instructions for how to terminate the rest of the angel kin were outlined at the top. The instructions for York, however, were annotated and on an attachment Gallagher did not have. I, on the other hand, knew exactly what was in store for us. Lucifer had sent me a litany of promises that made me shiver. If I had said yes to helping him get what he wanted, the entire world would have fallen into dark times, but my family would be left unharmed.

Instead, I had stood on the side of the angels and now my wife was dead, along with a dozen angel descendants.

I scanned the list and moved to turn the page but stalled at a name I recognized in New York City. I glanced at Steve, holding the list so he could see the name, and his gaze shot to mine. We ran into that descendant by chance, and I'd have to remember to warn him if I ever got out of this jam.

The crossed off names corresponded to the deaths, and I finally glanced up at the Chief, handing the list back.

"That looks like a hit list," I said, playing the game the way Steve was silently directing me to.

"That's a pretty damned expansive list, and the only names in this town are related to you in some way. Why is York tagged as last?"

"I don't know." I really didn't understand the logic of Lucifer's logistical orders. First, last, what did it matter? Then the answer came like a sucker punch to the stomach. Any chance of another CJ or Grace was limited to right here in York. If either Valerie or Naomi had another girl, the odds of Lucifer getting his hands on a trinity to create his dark army increased.

I closed my eyes and dropped my head.

"You're lying to me again."

I glanced up at him. How could I tell this man the devil existed, and he wanted both CJ and me dead, or using one of our super-powered meat suits to get what he wanted?

"Duke, are you going to process him or not?" Steve interrupted, reading my hesitation correctly.

"Whose hit list is this?" He waved the list before slamming it back on top of the file.

"Lucifer," I said, and the space between his eyebrows creased.

"Come again?"

I kept my hands still and just stared at him. "I run a paranormal investigation agency. I was bound to piss off the wrong... entity... at some point," I finally said. I knew how flippant that sounded, but it was easier to point to my job as the culprit than the truth. The truth could get me locked up in an uncomfortably small padded cell.

His eyebrows arched in surprise. It was something he hadn't considered, especially since he thought paranormal was complete bullshit.

I shifted. "If you're not going to process me, can I please go back to the hospital? I don't want my daughter waking up without me there."

His lips thinned. "You never explained all of your miraculous recoveries."

"I stopped the debris from hitting me," I said.

"How?"

"Psychic, remember?" I tapped my temple. The exhaustion of the last few days was taking its toll, and I knew it wasn't prudent to get snarky, but at this point, I was beyond caring.

"Bullshit," he said, and his thoughts circled back to me being a part of all of it.

I had had enough and moved forward, slamming my palm to his forehead. The memory transfer took a few minutes, and I'm sure revealing everything from the point we pulled in until the point I caught Hannah in my arms was going to haunt me but it would at least shut off this circle of questions, and I really wanted to get back to my daughter.

His incessant blinking pulled a huff out of me. Served him right for pushing me, and Steve just sent me an 'are you kidding me?' stare.

Finally, Chief Gallagher's eyes focused on me. "How much of that was real?"

"Unless you are going to tell me my wife is alive, and I just hallucinated her death, it's all real."

"What the hell did you just do to me? Was that some kind of hypnosis?" Gallagher snapped.

"No. I just shared the memory. It's part of my psychic charm." I snapped and the snarky remark earned a huff from both Gallagher and Steve.

Gallagher's eyes narrowed as he glared at me. "There was no explanation in that memory as to how the hell your daughter and Steve walked out alive," he muttered.

"Look, sir, I figured it was the fastest way for you to see what went down and as far as how we are alive, chalk that up to a miracle. Now, if you don't mind, I'd really like to get back to my daughter."

"Is my client free to go?" Steve asked and Chief Gallagher glanced down at the file with the information he used to get a warrant.

"One last question. When was the last time you were in your office?"

"The end of June. We usually close the first two weeks in July for summer vacation."

"So, you haven't been on your computer since then?"

I shook my head. "I always shut it down before I leave and lock it in my drawer."

"The laptop was on your desk and in sleep mode. Are you sure you haven't used it since June?"

"I locked it in my desk drawer before I left for vacation," I reiterated and my teeth clenched at the sudden rise in anger that overcame me. "Did you check to see if there were any signs of a break in, or did you just assume it was me that did all this and to hell with due process?" I growled and glanced at Steve.

He put his hand out to calm the beginnings of my rant.

"Did you check?" Steve asked.

Gallagher shook his head. "No. But I will have them check both the office door and the desk for signs of tampering," he said, appeasing my aggravation for the time being. Even with all he had been privy to, he still carried some doubt about me.

If the table was turned, I'm not sure I could swallow this either, but I was too tired to be sympathetic to his confusion.

"Can I go back to the hospital now?"

He studied me for a few minutes and then straightened up the notes in his folder before he nodded. "I'm not going to hold you in custody. But until we come to a solid conclusion on this case, I don't want you to leave town. Got it?"

"I got it." I stood, letting Steve walk me out to his car.

"You'll get me a copy of the case file once they close the case, right?" I asked, as I slid into the passenger seat.

"Why?"

I met his gaze. He of all people should understand my need for information.

I needed to know what happened.

I needed to know how long Raven suffered while we dicked around trying to find her.

I needed to know just how deeply I had failed her.

MY DAYS BLENDED TOGETHER while Hannah remained in a coma.

Gallagher had been in to talk to me a few more times since he hauled me into the station, but since they had found signs of a break in at my office, they had dropped all charges. Relief wrapped around me, easing my fear of having to leave Hannah's side for more than a few hours. She was vulnerable here and her name was still on that hit list.

Gallagher's questions now centered on the why, and if I thought there would be more deaths based on the hit list. I did not believe this was over, as a matter of fact I thought it was just the beginning, and I made my thoughts on the matter crystal-clear.

I also told him he needed to warn the others on the list because someone eventually would come for them.

They identified the killer. His name was Scout McHenry, a former Special Forces operative who was dishonorably discharged, and had a criminal record a mile long, including assault, battery, and petty larceny. He was a known mercenary, and from the little bits I was able to pull from Gallagher's mind, it seemed he had a group of friends that held themselves out in the same manner.

My mind kept returning to the ghost and what he said, and it seemed he wasn't bullshitting me in the least. There were plenty of others like him, willing to finish the job.

Gallagher stationed a plain-clothes cop outside the hospital room in response to my reasoning and I'm not entirely sure if it was for my daughter's safety or just to keep an eye on me. The glimpse he had of what happened was enough to make him wary of me, and of what I could do. He wasn't sure about Steve either, but he had the impression I held the power of the universe at my fingertips, which wasn't far from the truth.

I didn't quite understand his frequent visits. It was as if he kept having to validate the truth by seeing the results over and over again. It took a week to close the case and clear my name and my daughter still hadn't woken up.

I stared out the window, ignoring Raven's ghost when the knock came on the door. I turned, meeting Gallagher's gaze as he poked his head in once again.

"Any change?" he asked with genuine concern.

I shook my head. "Unfortunately, no."

"Do you have a second?" he asked, stepping in the room.

"Sure," I said, turning my focus towards him.

He closed the door behind him and crossed to the end of Hannah's bed. His hands fidgeted and he let out a small nervous laugh. "I've been turning over all the things you fed into my head for days now and I need to ask you a question," he started and cleared his throat.

I gave him a nod, waiting. He now had my entire attention and the flurry of thought in his mind only allowed for a few broken words to bleed through.

"Are you... from here?" he asked, and my eyebrows rose.

"You know I was born in York," I said and refrained from adding more because the words I was getting were laughable and all related to Superman or some other insane superhero reference from outer space.

He glanced at the floor and shoved his hands in his pockets. "I know, but were your parents..." He trailed off, shifting his weight and I pressed my lips against a smirk.

When I was sure I wouldn't laugh in his face, I said, "I'm human, Chief. So were my parents."

He looked up at me and his cheeks turned red with embarrassment.

"I'm just a little more supercharged than most," I added and this time I couldn't wipe the grin from my face.

He let out a nervous laugh, shuffling his feet.

"And I get the distinct impression you didn't come here just to ask me if I was from another solar system," I said, yanking his chain. It had the desired effect. This time his laughter was more natural, and he pointed his finger at me.

"You got me there, son. I came because even with the odd questions rolling around in my mind, I think you'd make a hell of an officer. We certainly could use someone with your talents on the force."

I stared at him and now that his mind had cleared, I was able to evaluate his motives and it wasn't to keep an eye on me. It was a genuine offer. One I had never in my wildest dreams considered.

"Are you seriously offering me a job?" I asked, laughing. "After all the trouble I got into when I was younger?"

He joined me, chuckling as he pulled his hands out of his pocket. "You certainly were a piece of work. And yes, I am offering you a position on the force."

I glanced at my daughter and sighed. I knew what kind of demands a cop's life entailed and while York was fairly quiet in the crime department, the hours away when things went to hell wasn't something I was willing to do. Not now that I was Hannah's only surviving parent.

"It's a quiet town," he added as if he knew my current thought process.

I turned to him. "I appreciate the offer, but I've got the paranormal investigation agency and I have the freedom of dictating my own hours. I can't give that up right now. Especially with everything that's happened. Hannah is going to need me when she wakes up."

His calm exhale and nod told me he knew it was a long shot. "I figured. But I had to give it a try. I also came by to let you know O'Keefe's memorial service is scheduled for Friday."

My smile faded. "I'll do my best to be there, but it all depends on my daughter," I said. "And I'll let Steve and CJ know. I'm sure they'll want to make an appearance."

"I appreciate that," he said and turned to leave.

"Chief?"

He half turned back, meeting my gaze.

"If you ever need help with a case in the future..."

"I know where to find you," he said with a nod.

I watched him go, and for the first time, I felt at ease with the cops in this town. We had a long adversarial history, but for some reason, this time, the hatchet was buried, and I'd earned a little respect from the top. It was a good feeling, even though I could never see myself as a small-town cop.

I glanced over at Raven and she stood with her arms crossed, looking at me through her upper lashes like I was in the doghouse.

"What?" I said to her.

"You would make a fantastic cop. You should have taken that job."

"I don't need to work at all," I said, crossing my arms in response. "Besides, I lived the life of a cop's son. I'm not doing that to Hannah."

Her arms dropped, along with her attitude and her sigh ruffled the bed covers. Both our gazes dropped to Hannah. She was more important than a job.

Besides, I now had another goal. I needed to make Lucifer pay for what he did to my family.

Chapter 23

I SHIFTED IN THE chair, and my back muscles clenched in response, sending a sharp pain up my spine and I sat up, glancing at the morning sunrise from the window. Hannah still slept peacefully and Raven still stood watch.

I crossed to the john to relieve my bladder and splash some water on my face. It had been over a week now, and I doubted the possibility of her waking up, even with Valerie's magic. I sported the start of a serious beard, and I glanced in the mirror at the door where Raven's ghost leaned on the doorjamb like she was waiting to impart some level of wisdom. But she remained silent.

I had prayed more in the last few days than I have since I was locked in that butcher's garage in Georgia. I begged God and the heavens to make my daughter forget the horrors she saw. I didn't want her to remember her mother that way. I knew all too well what that does to a person's head.

Steve came by for a few minutes last night to bring me another change of clothes, and he had the copy of the police report for me. I told him about the memorial service, but neglected to tell him Gallagher offered me a job on the force.

I'm not sure what his take would have been, but I knew he would understand my rationale. Besides, I didn't need the money, not with the millions already in my name.

The report still sat on the side table, unread. Every time I reached for it, Raven intervened, asking me not to. She didn't want me to know what he did to her, but I needed to know. I saw enough on the video to give me nightmares for the rest of my life, but I needed the clinical assessment.

I crossed from the bathroom and took a seat next to the bed, staring at the report once again. I moved aside the necklace and her wedding rings that Steve had delivered along with the file and reached for the folder.

"Please don't."

I glanced at Raven's ghost standing on the other side of the bed and hesitated. Her hair shimmered red, as if a band of sunshine now lived in the strands. She was beyond beautiful, and I sighed, pulling my hand back.

"Why didn't you try to contact me?" I asked. The question ate at me, and I finally found the courage to ask her. Everyone in the family knew how to send a mental SOS, but she never even made a peep.

"I was too worried about Hannah to focus enough to send a message out, and then I was in too much pain to form a thought." Her gaze dropped to the floor in shame.

I closed my eyes with a sigh and then turned, reaching for the file, despite her protests.

"Babe, I need to know," I said, meeting her gaze before I opened the file.

Just like the reports O'Keefe showed me earlier this week, the folder began with photos, and I glanced at her, turning them over to give her some level of comfort and her protests calmed. She didn't know I had seen the beginning of the video, and her rationale was focused on the images, but it was already there, just behind my eyelids. The pictures couldn't do any more damage than was already done.

I focused on the notes. Words were easier to digest and keep the reality at bay for a little longer, but the details outlined in the autopsy swept a layer of ice over my skin.

Raven had been full of bloodstone from her esophagus to her anus, so full, in fact, that her intestines perforated in multiple places and her stomach had lacerations as well. The bastard had sewn her shut so the stone would do more damage than the insertion had. The leakage of stomach acid and intestinal bacteria into her abdominal cavity had already formed infection, and she had transitioned into a state of septic shock. If the spear hadn't punctured her heart, the damage was so widespread that she would have died within hours, anyway.

Even if Valerie healed her, the stones would have continued to tear her to pieces from the inside out.

I scanned the next paragraph. Not only was her digestive track full, but her sexual organs were also filled with the sharp shards. The next sentence made my eyes dart to Raven's and the pain in the center of my chest spread.

"You were pregnant?"

She bit her lip. I didn't think ghosts could cry, but a teardrop leaked from the corner of her eye, tumbling down her cheek like a glass prism. When she nodded, I dropped the file on the floor and folded my arms on the side of Hannah's bed before I buried my face in the crook of my elbow.

My loss hit all at once and the tears came in a torrent of shaking sobs. It wasn't until a warm hand landed on the back of my neck that I realized I wasn't alone in my misery. I glanced up, right into my daughter's deep blue eyes and she smiled.

"It's going to be okay, Daddy," she said in that small and innocent voice and then she looked straight at the ghost of my wife and said, "Right, Mommy?"

My daughter carried my affinity for seeing ghosts, and I wondered if she had her mother's natural gift for witchcraft. Wiping my face on the edge of the sheet, I straightened and forced a smile to my lips, sweeping her into my arms in a big bear hug.

I glanced at Raven and she gave me a weak smile.

When I released Hannah, Raven leaned in and planted a soft kiss on her forehead. "You be good for your father."

Hannah's smile faded, and she blinked in confusion, like she recognized her mother wasn't solid. She was more like a wisp of smoke, instead.

"Mommy has to go, but your dad knows a special place where you can come visit me whenever you need me. Okay?"

Hannah glanced at me.

"Paradise Cove," I said. It was a place I wanted to make camp for the rest of my life now that it was the only way to see or feel Raven again.

Hannah stared at me, her eyes widening.

"Daddy can talk," she pointed at me and looked at Raven.

My wife smiled. "Yes. That was the last gift I could give him." Raven leaned close to Hannah. "Make sure your daddy finds another someone special. I don't want him to be alone for the rest of his life, okay?"

I sent my best 'you're out of your fucking mind' glare at the ghost and then met my daughter's wide-eyed gaze.

Raven leaned across the bed and planted a soft kiss on my cheek. "Love you, always," she whispered.

"Love you, too," I said, and Raven's solid form turned to smoke, wrapping around the two of us before dissolving to nothing. "Always."

I kept Hannah's gaze even as the emptiness swallowed my soul.

"I guess Mommy waited until you were awake to say goodbye," I said, softly.

Hannah's chin trembled, and I reached for the necklace on the table, bringing the beautiful Celtic knot into view.

"She left this for you," I said and slipped it over her head, giving her a piece of her mother's magical protection that had done nothing to prevent her demise.

Hannah pressed it to her chest and then reached for me like she understood just how much I needed a hug. At this moment, she reminded me more of Grace than my little ball of unending energy, but I accepted the hug, along with the fact that perhaps the angel blood coursing through our veins made us a little stronger than we had a right to be.

The End

Continue Tom's story with Angel Fire.

About J.E. Taylor

J.E. Taylor is a USA Today bestselling author, a publisher, an editor, a manuscript formatter, a mother, a wife, a business analyst, and a Supernatural fangirl. Not necessarily in that order. She first sat down to seriously write in February of 2007 after her daughter asked:

> "Mom, if you could do anything, what would you do?"

> From that moment on, she hasn't looked back.

Besides being co-owner of Novel Concept Publishing, Ms. Taylor also moonlights as a Senior Editor of Allegory E-zine, an online venue for Science Fiction, Fantasy and Horror, and co-host of the popular YouTube talk show Spilling Ink.

She lives in New Hampshire with her husband and during the summer months enjoys her weekends on the shore in southern Maine.

Visit her at www.jetaylor75.com to check out her other titles.

If you liked ANGEL BLOOD, check out the rest of THE
RYAN CHRONICLES:

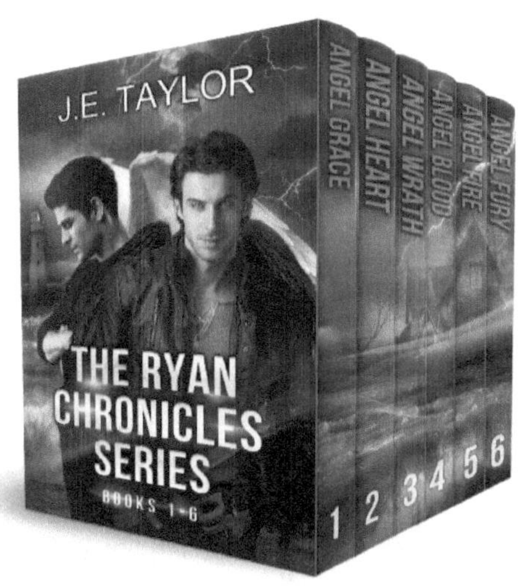

THE RYAN CHRONICLES

**Demons, vampires, angels, and the devil.
What the hell kind of nightmare do I live in?**

CJ Ryan was born with enough psychic power to
destroy the earth. And Lucifer wants him to do just
that.

Raised with a strong moral compass, CJ won't
sacrifice innocent lives to protect his own, and that
puts him at odds with the devil.

But if he doesn't give in, he and all he loves will
become the target of Lucifer's rage.

When CJ gives his twin brother, Tom, a dose of his
powers to keep him safe, it puts Tom directly in
Lucifer's crosshairs.

As the final battle draws near, what will they have to sacrifice to keep their loved ones safe?

Can they survive the devil's wrath?

THE RYAN CHRONICLES includes these titles:

CJ's Story:

ANGEL GRACE - Book 1

ANGEL HEART - Book 2

ANGEL WRATH – Book 3

Tom's Story:

ANGEL BLOOD - Book 4

ANGEL FIRE - Book 5

ANGEL FURY – Book 6

Fans of Supernatural and Shadowhunters will enjoy this series.

You might also like the GAMES THRILLER SERIES which highlights CJ and Tom's parents and their unorthodox history together.

GAMES THRILLER SERIES

Intensely disturbing. Beautifully horrific. Indescribably intense.

When Ty Aris kidnaps Jessica Connor for his stepbrother's underground film network, he is not prepared for the impact she has on him.

His obsession with her lights a fire under his ass to get out of the ungodly business with his stepbrother.

But the only way to leave the business is in a body bag.

In the dark plane between life and death, Ty is given a choice: save his soulmate or save his very soul.

The Games Thriller Series includes:

Fallen – A Games Series Prequel

Survival Games

Mind Games

End Game

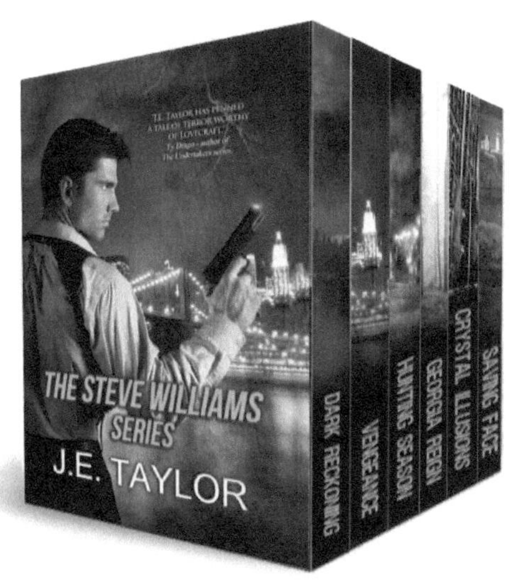

THE STEVE WILLIAMS SERIES

Special Agent Steve Williams excels at his job, catching the most heinous of monsters walking the earth.

Serial killers.

When his job brings him face to face with a psychic, he struggles to accept her gifts in his neat little black and white world. Armed with her visions, along with his skills as an FBI agent, he hunts the worst of the worst, but will he catch the killer before they set their sights on him?

Unstoppable, breath stealing, and terrifying all at once.

Gripping, rich and magnificent!

275

The Steve Williams Series mixes compelling crime thrillers with supernatural forces that will grip the reader from page one. This six-book series takes you through some of Steve Williams' darkest cases in his FBI career.

The STEVE WILLIAMS SERIES includes Dark Reckoning, Vengeance, Hunting Season, Georgia Reign, Crystal Illusions, and Saving Face.

Find these titles and other fantasy and suspense titles on J.E. Taylor's website!

www.JETaylor75.com